MELISSA ADDEY

The
Cup

The Cup

First Paperback Print Edition: 2018 in United Kingdom

The moral right of the author has been asserted.

Published by Letterpress Publishing

Cover and Formatting: Streetlight Graphics

Map of the Almoravid empire by Maria Gandolfo

www.melissaaddey.com

Paperback ISBN: 978-1-910940-45-7
Kindle ISBN: 978-1-910940-44-0

For Ben

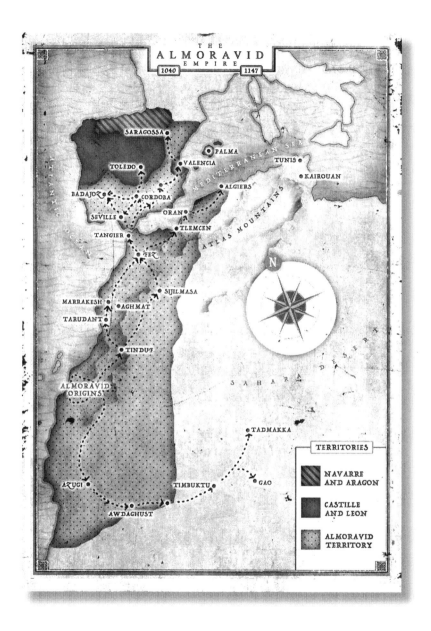

THE
ALMORAVID
EMPIRE
1040   1147

SARAGOSSA
PALMA
VALENCIA   TUNIS
TOLEDO   KAIROUAN
MEDITERRANEAN SEA
BADAJOZ   CORDOBA   ALGIERS
SEVILLE   ORAN
TANGIER   TLEMCEN
ATLAS MOUNTAINS
FEZ
SIJILMASA
MARRAKESH   AGHMAT
TARUDANT
TINDUF
ALMORAVID
ORIGINS
SAHARA DESERT
TADMAKKA
AZUGI   TIMBUKTU   GAO
AWDAGHUST

N

TERRITORIES

NAVARRE
AND ARAGON

CASTILLE
AND LEON

ALMORAVID
TERRITORY

Black Feathers

They were so bright, these feathers. So bright. She loved the birds, perhaps they were easier for her to love than her husband, her daughter. The birds made her smile, a rare sight. Their chirrups and songs lightened our heavy house.

I wander the rooms, returning again and again to their cages. They could not escape their fate and perhaps neither can I. Now their feathers are black with the force of the fire and when I touch them they crumble beneath my fingertips, ashes falling to meet the ashes on the floor.

I did not mean for this to happen. I was a child with powers too great for a child when this began. I am not even sure when all this began, whether it was one moment or another.

My father was a trader of slaves when I was given the cup. That is as much of a beginning as I can be sure of.

The city of Kairouan, Tunisia

c. 1020

The Slave Woman

LAVES SHOULD NOT BE SOLD in the hottest part of the day, they tremble on the block or sometimes faint away and no-one will buy a slave who shows signs of weakness. Besides, the customers grow weary of standing in the heat themselves and are unlikely to buy, growing ill-tempered and tight fisted. The heat today is reaching its zenith and my father is anxious to finish his work for the day and retire for food and drink.

"A fine man! Broad shoulders, calloused hands. Long legs. A good worker sir, he will serve you well."

There is a pause while my father watches his customer's face as he inspects the slave. Standing by his side I murmur something and my father pretends to give me water to drink, the better to hear me.

"He is afraid," I say, speaking directly into my father's ear. "A slave beat him once."

My father does not change expression, nor ask how I know. He pats me on the head before speaking loudly. "Be off with you, stop pestering me now, Hela. I have business to attend to." I move away and become wholly engrossed with a doll, a ragged little thing I have very little interest in. My father's camel whooshes in my ear and I slap its hairy face and stinking breath away from me.

My father turns back to his customer. "Of course, one must be careful with such an ox of a man that he has also a good temperament," he says. "One cannot be too careful." Without warning, he cuffs the slave's head. The unexpected blow causes him to stagger. He regains his stance looking a little bewildered but shows no sign of anger. I watch the customer's face relax in relief and know that my father has made a sale.

He makes many more sales that morning. A slave girl of unusual good looks to a man filled with lust, a giant of a slave to a man convinced his enemies are trying to kill him, a rounded slave woman suckling a child to a household where the mother needs a wet-nurse. Each time a slave is brought to the block I find some way to draw my father's attention to the person in the crowd most likely to pay a high price.

I feel them. I feel their desires, their needs, I feel their fears and hopes. I sense what they feel when they gaze at my father's wares, the silent men and women whose lives hang in the balance, their destinies chosen by me, a child barely ten years' old.

I feel the slaves as well, if they have feelings. Some of them do not. Their feelings have been buried somewhere so deep I cannot touch them, cannot penetrate beyond the numbness that fills the space where they should be. Sometimes I will feel their shriveled hopes and fulfil them if I can, a frightened and broken woman going to a lonely old mistress rather than a hard master. But I am a child and mostly I think of my father's profits and the little gifts he will give me if I choose well for him. When a customer pays more than a slave is worth because of their own desires, then my father will nod to me and I know that I will be rewarded. Perhaps with a fine leather belt, a sweetmeat, once even a kitten of my own. My father says that when I am a grown woman I should marry a slave trader myself, for I will undoubtedly bring him much success in his business. To my mother, when she enquires, he tells her in good humour that I am no trouble to him at all, that I may play nearby when the slave auctions are held and she smiles, thinking him a kindly man for indulging his little daughter's fondness for being near him. She does remind him, though, that as a girl, my place is with my mother and that one day soon I must learn her trade.

My mother is a quiet woman, a skilled woman. A wise woman. Her rooms are silent and cool, nothing like the heat and noise of the slave market. Neat jars line the walls, her pestles and mortars below them, ranked by size and use. Some may be used for more than one purpose, others are set far back and used for only one ingredient, for even their taint could be dangerous.

It is mostly other women who come to my mother. They enter hesitantly, greet her with respect and a little fear, whisper their needs. Sometimes my mother nods and bids them return another time for what they seek and they will disappear. Sometimes, if she can make what they ask for quickly, she will tell them they may wait. They do so, squatting by the door, as far away from her as they can manage. They watch her with hope as she chooses and grinds, mixes and pours. They look about them with awe at the myriad containers and most of all at the books.

My mother can read, a rare skill for a woman. She reads slowly, one arm cradling the heavy tomes, one finger tracing the words. Sometimes I see her struggle to mouth a new name. She spends time looking at the illustrations, nodding to herself at the uses for leaves, stems, roots, flowers and berries, seeds. She can write too, in a careful hand, each stroke laborious. She is careful because her little jars must not be confused one with another.

Sometimes I watch her when she is grinding herbs, but it seems dull work and I flit away soon enough, back to the noise and smells of the market.

Now there is only one slave left to sell. My father pursed his lips when he saw her and muttered under his breath. She is twisted, one shoulder higher than the other. Her body is scrawny, no tempting curves here to sate a man's desire. The few clothes she wears are mere scraps and at her waist she carries some kind of pouched bag, badly made from reddish leather. Where the other slaves stood still and silent behind the block, awaiting their turn to stand on it, their eyes cast down, the woman sits hunched up on the ground, her head twisting this way and that. Occasionally I hear words coming from her but she hails from the Dark Kingdom and I do not understand her. My father glances at me when he sees me looking at her and I shrug. I cannot feel her own desires and so I must think of who might want her, must spot them in the crowd and feel their need for her.

But when she mounts the block there is nothing in the

crowd, already fast-dwindling. The woman limps when she walks, not a small limp but a strange, whole-body lurching. She would barely be able to carry water without it spilling. She may not sell at all and if she does not my father will be angry, he has no use for slaves who do not make him money. She stands for a moment and then sinks to a low crouch, my father cuffs her but she will not stand again.

My father tries to entice the crowd forwards. "She's strong enough," he says. "I've had bigger, stronger women die on the journey here, but I never heard a whimper from her. She may be a cripple but that won't stop her working. Might stop her running off though, eh?" he smiles.

The crowd begins to drift away. My father names a price for her but only receives shaking heads as a reply.

I look about me and spot one of the tannery-masters. I tug at my father's robe and he nods, climbs down from the block where he has been standing and joins the master, speaks smilingly with him. Anyone who works in the tanneries is likely to die soon enough, their skin scarred and burnt by the foul vats of stinking mess they use to soften and dye animal skins. It's a hard life, carrying heavy pails of bird droppings, water, lime and ash, your back bent beneath the burning heat of the sun, your legs trembling from the endless stamping down of the skins in the skin-stripping liquid. The tannery master buys plenty of slaves at a knock-down price: the old, the crippled, the mute or stupid and uses up what is left of their broken lives. My father does not usually sell much to them, for he prefers a better quality of stock but on this occasion he has been let down and he is not about to waste much time on such an unlikely proposition. I see the negotiations going on between them while closer to us the crowd has dispersed entirely.

I'm growing hungry and my father could be a while. If I set off now I will be home ahead of him to warn our household to prepare a meal. My mouth waters at the thought of fresh hot flatbreads dipped into *lablabi,* a thick soup of chickpeas and garlic, or perhaps wrapped around slices of spiced sausage. Maybe my mother will have made sweet *samsa*, nuts and pastry flavoured with rosewater syrup. If she has it is probably still cooling, made for the evening meal but I might beg some from her while it is still warm. I stand up.

"Girl."

I turn, surprised. The old cripple has spoken in my own language. "You can speak?"

She shakes her head. "Little." Her voice croaks, as though she has not spoken for a long time or is desperate for water. Either is possible.

I shrug. "You'll learn. You don't need many words at the tanneries."

She makes a slow gesture, a beckoning.

I step closer to her. I am not wary. My father is close by and what harm can she do me?

She is scrabbling about in the red pouch, searching for something among her meagre belongings. At last she pulls something from its depths and holds it out to me. It is a cup made of a dark carved wood, the carvings rough and not very clear, for the cup looks to have been used for many years, so that what were once sharply etched images are now almost smoothed away by the touch of many hands. It has been stained red at some time, but again the redness has been worn away, leaving it mottled here and there.

I look at her without touching the cup. "Your new master will give you water when you reach your home," I tell her, miming drinking and pointing to the tannery master, who is now nodding agreement with my father.

But she becomes agitated, perhaps realising she does not have a lot of time left before her new master will claim her. She thrusts the cup towards me and I reach out and take it, one finger brushing her skin as I do so.

The jolt knocks me to the ground. I lie there, clutching the cup to me, rage and an unholy power flowing through me as though I am possessed by a djinn. Above me the woman lurches to her feet and looks down on me over her twisted shoulder. Her eyes fix on mine and I whimper and wriggle away from her, but I do not let go of the cup. I have never sensed such feelings from a slave, nor even from any free-born man or woman. I have felt the uncontrolled rage of small children, stamping their feet at some perceived outrage, I have felt the power emanating from desert warriors but this... this is a rage that would make a grown man kneel in fear, a power that would topple kings. How can a crippled slave woman possess either? I stare up at her and she points at the cup.

"Yours," she rasps and then she smiles. It is a crippled smile, like her body, a lopsided thing that does not offer comfort.

I have spent the rest of my life wondering about her smile at that moment, whether she saw my abilities and meant to give me a gift or whether the cup was a curse on me for sending her to the tanneries.

I am still not sure.

My father rejoins us and does not notice anything amiss. I am upright again and the cup has disappeared into my own bag, a cheerful thing of yellow leather, a previous gift for my services. The slave woman is led away and although I watch her every step she never once looks back as she follows her new master across the square and into the dark souk beyond.

The next time I accompany my father I do not tell him anything useful, nor the time after that. I am wary of the slaves now, I do not trust the numbness that is in them. I am afraid of what they may do to me if I send them towards a bleak destiny and there are not many destinies I could choose that would not be bleak in one way or another. And so I am silent until finally he tells my mother, not unkindly, that it is time I learnt her trade, he cannot have a half-grown girl loitering near the slave block, it is not proper at my age. I must learn her trade and then I will be married.

My Mother's Rooms

Even my mother is startled by how fast I learn her skills.

I learn to read at a pace that astonishes her and yet it is her jars that help me. I have only to unstopper one, to smell its contents and look at the label, the shapes marked there coming to mean that smell so that even now, I can read a word and at once inhale its scent from the empty air. My mother teaches me to read as she does everything: with a slow care but when she sees how fast I outstrip her, how I do not need to trace each stroke to know its sound, she allows me to touch her precious books and soon enough it becomes my task to read aloud to her.

She only has to tell me once the properties and uses of a plant and I remember it. She tests me over and over again, uncertain whether I have been lucky in my guesses, whether perhaps I have cheated her in some way but eventually she accepts that my memory does not lie. It takes her a while, however, to notice my other skills.

"Why did you give her that?" I ask.

My mother looks up. Her patient has left us, clutching a small pot to her. "The swelling may be helped by the application."

"But she is dying," I say, with all the hard truth of a child's tongue.

My mother gazes at me for a long time. "Why do you say that?"

"She smells sick," I say.

My mother's eyes narrow. "Smells?"

I nod, shrugging. Surely my mother can smell what I smelt? "It made me feel ill," I say. "It was like honey mixed with rotting meat."

My mother does not reply. But after each patient visits her, she looks to me and asks, "What did they smell of?"

Sometimes they smell of the food they have been cooking, or of the black olive soap from the hammams, sometimes of the rose perfume that Kairouan is famous for. Sometimes I smell the strange smell again. But I smell other things. I smell fear, happiness, despair. I smell anger, need, desire. Each has its own smell and sometimes it is so strong I cannot stand it and have to open the windows in my mother's room. When I do this she watches me and then she speaks with more care to her visitors, asks them more questions, until, often, they tell her what I had already scented in the air: their fear of a husband's fists or his belt, their desire for a person forbidden to them, their desperate need for a child to hold in their arms. They come for minor ailments, but they soon confess to greater wounds.

"You have been given a gift," says my mother, and she does not say it with smiling praise for her little daughter, she says it with the respect due to a fellow healer and perhaps a little fear at how easily her own skills fade beside me. Perhaps she expects me to show some pride, even arrogance at how easily I learn her skills, but when she says 'gift' I think only of the slave woman's cup, hidden in my room and I fall silent and bow my head.

Now a little room is set aside for me beside my mother's and here I am made to grind down roots and leaves, to preserve berries and flower petals. I take my place beside my mother when her patients visit and listen to their whispered confessions or groaning complaints. My mother will look to me, to see what I suggest, and I will stand before the tiny jars and choose one and another and my mother will nod, perhaps point to a third, or shake her head a little and suggest another choice. But she does not often have to correct me, as time goes by.

We visit the souk together and wander its narrow mazelike streets to find the stallholders who keep the items we need. Fenugreek, to make a woman's breasts swell with milk. Argan oil to make blood flow within the body more freely, black cumin to father a child. Sometimes we go to meet traders who are newly arrived in one of Kairouan's many caravanserai. They bring fresh supplies of ingredients but also powerful amulets and living plants for my mother's herb garden, which I learn to tend. The courtyard of our home is stacked everywhere with pots of plants that the slave girls are not permitted to touch, for some can bring death. Only my mother and I may care for them.

When I am free of tasks, I pore over my mother's books. She has only three, but they are huge and beautiful and she treasures them. Sometimes I take up her reed pen and try to draw what I see, the shapes of leaves, the petals curved like so, the tiny roots like hairs, creeping across the page. My mother nods at my efforts and allows me more paper, even though it is costly, as well as ink, although I have to make my own supplies, from the burnt-up wool and horns of sheep.

She allows me to sit in her place, to hear her patients' stories and they look startled at such a young girl taking on her mother's work so soon, but she only says, "She has a great talent, greater than mine," and they hurry to agree, hoping that perhaps there is healing in my hands.

When the first headache comes, I think I am going to die. The pain is so great that I cannot stand. I stagger to my room and fall onto my bed, my mother following me.

"My head," I say, and I can hardly speak above a whisper.

My mother makes the room dark, gives me the correct herbs, holds cooling cloths to my head and murmurs words of prayer. But the pain goes on so long I begin to weep. It feels as though a giant has a hold of my head and is slowly trying to pull it apart, as my father can split a ripe pomegranate in two with his bare hands.

The pain goes on and on. I try to sleep but it is impossible. At last there is a faint lessening and I cry again, from relief.

It is my mother, older and wiser than I, who notices the pattern after a while.

"Do the women's pains enter you, Hela?" she asks.

"When they are afraid I feel the fear," I tell her.

"And all their other feelings?"

I nod.

My mother sighs. "Too much for one body, to sense the

I nod and she sits in front of me. Hesitantly, she confesses that she has been unable to have children, even though she is of fertile stock and young. She is afraid that her husband, whom she loves, will turn away his gaze and bring home another wife if she cannot bear him a child.

It is a common enough complaint and I have barely finished listening to her when I am already collecting the right jars and bottles to mix her a draught which she must take each day. It does not always work but occasionally a woman bears a child after she has seen us and so they all come. My mother shakes her head when we are alone and says that only Allah can grant a child. Still, I grind the ingredients, mix up the concoction until it has the right consistency and bottle most of it. The first draught, she must take now. I look about me for a cup but the only one to hand is the carved cup. I hesitate for a moment but, feeling her questioning gaze, I take it and pour the drink into the cup before passing it to her.

As our hands touch the woman gasps. The cup rocks, neither of us willing to hold it alone until I slowly release my grip and the woman holds it, her eyes wide.

"What did you do?" she asks. "I saw a baby in my arms, I heard it cry and knew it was mine."

I shake my head. "I do not know," I say truthfully. "It must be that your desire for a child is very strong." I improvise. "Drink," I add.

The woman nods and quickly drinks every drop, clutching at the cup as though she is afraid that the brew's efficacy will go if she hesitates.

When she has gone I turn the cup over in my hands and wonder at what has happened. I wash it with care and replace it on the shelf. I do not use it again. I have so many others, I excuse myself.

But the young woman is back when less than two moons have passed and she brings me more silver than I have ever been paid.

"I am with child," she says. "My husband sent you this. He says he is the happiest man in Kairouan. He smiles all day."

I take the silver and murmur something in reply, I am not sure what.

"It was the red cup, wasn't it?" she says, looking eagerly up at it on the shelf, where it has sat unused since her first visit. "It has a special power, does it not?"

I do not look at the cup behind me. "The herbs will have done you good," I say.

She nods and thanks me again and goes away but she has a busy mouth, for now one and then another woman asks if I will use 'the red cup' when I treat them. If I try to dissuade them, saying that one cup is much like another, they insist that they must drink from the cup.

And strange things happen when they do.

Often as I hand them the cup something passes between us, a shock as though a power jumps from one to the other, a pale copy of the jolt I felt from the slave woman so long ago.

One woman recovers even though my mother shook her head when she saw how ill she was and I had already smelt the smell of death upon her.

A child who had not spoken before speaks.

Woman upon woman finds herself with child when they had lost hope. My mother asks me what I give them and I shake my head and say that I give them what we have always given them. My mother frowns and says she has never known it to work so well. She asks about the red cup and I mumble something about it coming from the Dark Kingdom. My mother turns it in her hands but does not seem to feel anything when she does and shrugs, saying that it is my own healing abilities that the women are benefiting from and that their nonsense about a cup is only superstition. To which I do not reply.

By the time I am seventeen I have amassed a sum of silver that would mark me as rich, for a healer. Women give me their jewellery, their husbands send coins, as many as they can spare, for my name is now known across the city of Kairouan. Now it is my mother who grinds ingredients for me, who washes the pots and cups, the pestles and mortars, who tidies the workrooms. I am too busy, there is a never-ending line of people who wait, squatting on the stairs leading to my consulting room. And always, always, I must use the red cup or face their disappointment.

The Boy with the Red Lips

*1*T IS HIS LIPS I notice first. They are full and so red that the first time I see him I believe he has been hurt, that his lips are bleeding and that he is standing in my room to be healed. But it is his mother, a woman named Safa, that he has accompanied here. She is the wife of a copper merchant in the city. She wants some minor cure, for a cough or some such and I mix what is needed without knowing what I am doing, my hands moving alone from years of practice. When I let her sip from the cup she shudders. She rises to leave but I stop her, my hand on her richly decorated robes.

"You must come every day," I say. I can see she is wealthy, she will not baulk at the price.

"Is it worse than a cough, *Lalla*?" asks the woman fearfully, using the term of respect I have heard more and more often over the years.

"N-no," I say. "But I am giving you a new remedy. It must only be taken here, under my supervision. It is very efficacious," I add quickly. "You will be well very soon."

She leaves me murmuring thanks, which I do not hear. Every part of me is focused on her son, on his red lips.

Each day she comes and each day I see something else in him. His red lips give way to the darkness of his eyes, to his black curls, the golden-brown of his skin, the ripple of the muscles of his forearm when it emerges from beneath his robes to help his mother up. I do not know what I give his mother but when I see that she is indeed getting better I grow desperate. When she is well she will no longer come to me and nor will her son. He is strong and healthy. I may never see him again.

"A woman has asked for a love potion," I tell my mother, standing behind her while she cooks our dinner.

My mother laughs. "There is no such thing. Love comes when it wishes." My mother has never believed in such things although plenty of other healers offer love philtres and other, perhaps darker concoctions for those whose feelings have run away with them. Magic is part of most healers' work throughout the Maghreb and beyond, but my mother has always trusted only in her knowledge of plants, in the leaves and berries and roots. She says magic is not her place to know.

"But one could excite the pulses or quicken the heart," I say, thinking of my own heart and how it pounds when he stands near me.

My mother shakes her head. "It is not the same thing."

"Or excite the male member…" I say. I do not blush to say this as I should. I have spoken of such things many times. My face is pale with concentration.

My mother shrugs. "That is between a husband and wife," she says. "Does her husband have such difficulties?"

"I – I did not ask," I manage.

My mother makes a face that shows she does not think

very highly of me if I have not even asked such a simple question. "Tell her she must give you more information," she says and goes back to the cooking.

It is night and I do not sleep. I have not slept well for many days, since I first saw the shape of his lips, their blood-red curves. At last I get up from my bed and I make my way to the healing rooms. I open the shutters and a full moon lights the room so that I do not even light the lantern that I meant to use. The night air is cool and my half-naked body shivers.

I place a hand on one jar and then another. I smell their properties without removing the stoppers. I think what each will do when it enters the body, what they might do when mixed together. I do not take down the jars, only touch each one while in my mind the boy appears, his eyes lit up with desire, with love for me.

The next day before his mother arrives I make up her medicine and have it ready in a small bottle of its own. Then I take down the cup. I think of what it does, for I have had time to watch its work, these past years. I have come to believe that it intensifies the desire of the person who drinks from it, that whatever I mix takes on added power from their need for a child or a cure. The greater their desire, the more the cup makes powerful my own skills as a healer.

Now I turn the cup in my hands. I have never mixed anything inside the cup, I only pour into it what has already been made. What if I were to mix the potion I have in mind within the cup itself? Will it add to its power? Will my own desire affect the drink I make? I have never added my own desires to the cup, it has been my patients who have added theirs. Will my love, my lust, pass from me to him when he presses his lips against it and drinks?

As I mix together quantities from each bottle that I touched in the dark of moonlight last night I allow myself to think of him, to unleash the desire I feel for him into my fingers as I stir. At last, as I hear footsteps on the stairs leading to my room, I press my own lips against the cup. When I set it down, my hands shake.

Safa settles herself on the floor opposite me while her son gazes, bored, out of the window. I cannot help but admire his silhouette with the light behind him, each part of his profile outlined as though for my gaze alone.

Safa is all smiles. "I feel healthy again, *Lalla*," she tells me. "You are gifted."

"I am glad you are better," I manage. "I will give you one final draught and then you will be entirely well. But – but before you go I thought that perhaps your son should also drink a preventative. I would not want your cough to spread to other members of your household."

Safa looks a little surprised, glancing over her shoulder at her son. "Faheem? He is strong as an ox, but if you think it best…"

Faheem, I think. I had not known his name until now. *Faheem*. "Yes," I say, trying to keep my voice clear and firm. "He should have a mixture I have prepared. I am certain it will be good for him. One cannot be too careful."

Safa nods, "Of course. Drink this," she orders her son, waving towards the cup, which I am holding out.

Faheem steps forwards and takes the cup from me. One slender fingertip brushes mine and I rock back, placing my hands on the floor where no-one can see them shaking. The wave of desire I felt as we touched frightens me. It is what I feel for him but magnified so greatly that I want to snatch the cup back from him. It is too much, I think. Too much for one body to stand. But it is too late for me to countermand my own orders. His red lips press against where my own lips were moments ago and instead of a girl's foolish pleasure at the thought of it I feel my face draining of colour with fear. I take back the cup, wash it, fill it with Safa's innocuous mixture, watch her drink it. I do not hear her thanks, nor do I see Faheem's face as they leave, for I dare not raise my eyes.

If I had known that I would not see him again alive, perhaps I would have raised my eyes and looked once more at those red lips, perhaps I would have summoned every part of my boldness and traced them with one fingertip, the better to recall them when it was already too late to save him.

I hear nothing. Late at night I lie awake and wonder what I expect to hear. That Faheem has asked for my hand in marriage? His family is well off, the copper pots they make can be found in half the households of Kairouan. Would they even wish for such an alliance? Is he, even now, begging his father to relent and allow marriage to a healer? I hear him reminding them that I am not some purveyor of whispers and nonsense, mixtures of who knows what. I can read and write, I am known as the best healer in the city. My father is a slave trader, we have a comfortable home.

But days go by and I hear nothing. The moon wanes and rises full again and I hear nothing. I cannot bring myself to ask questions. I am silent. I do my work.

And then Safa arrives. Alone. Her face is drawn, she looks older than the last time I saw her, only a month ago.

"*Lalla,*" she sighs, settling in front of me. "I have need of your skills."

I try to swallow. "Ask and I will do all I can," I say, my voice croaking with a sudden dryness.

"My daughter Djalila refuses to be married. She will not eat. She grows thinner by the day and nothing we have done helps. After what has happened to us, my husband is distraught. He cannot lose another child."

I feel a terrible coldness settle on me. "What – what happened to your family?"

She looks at me wide-eyed. "You did not hear?"

I shake my head.

"My son Faheem, whom you saw when I came here before, he – he died."

I force my lips to move. "Died?"

She nods and her eyes fill. I wait while tears trickle down her face and she wipes them away. "He said his heart pounded, that his hands shook and his lips burnt. He died in less than a day. We thought it was a fever. I would have come to you, *Lalla,* for your healing hands but it was so quick."

My heart pounded for him, my hands shook at his red lips. Dark red wood against which I pressed my mouth. I take her hands, murmur the words that should be said, offering my condolences, meaningless words of comfort. I look into her eyes for blame and see nothing. Why should she suspect me, the best healer in Kairouan? Her only regret lies in not rushing for my aid.

I tell her that I am busy today but that tomorrow I will come to her house, meet with her daughter Djalila who refuses to leave her rooms. I embrace her, watch her wipe away more tears and escort her from my rooms back to a waiting servant who will accompany her home.

All of that day I mix and pour, speak words I no longer recall, watch as one mouth after another presses against the redness of the cup and when evening comes I make my excuses to my mother, tell her I do not feel like eating, retreat to my room.

The moon is bright again. I try to sleep but it wakes me again and again or maybe it is the dreams I do not have. I long for nightmares to punish me, to frighten me and yet there is nothing, only falling darkness when I sleep and the moon's too-bright gaze when I awake. At last I rise and make my way back to the healing rooms. I stand, naked and alone, staring at the red cup. When I throw it as hard as I can against the wall I expect to see it crack in two but it only falls to the floor, unharmed, its mottled red colour lit by moonshine. I am afraid to touch it again.

Djalila

1 KNOW THE PUNISHMENT FOR MURDER of course. I should pay *diyah*, blood money, to the family of Faheem and beg for their forgiveness, although they may refuse and ask instead for my death in recompense for their loss. If they grant me forgiveness then I should complete my atonement by undertaking to free a slave, feeding sixty poor people and keeping sixty fasts.

It does not seem enough. How can any of that be enough for taking Faheem's innocent life? How can my reckless desire be atoned for with mere fasting and feeding the poor? The silver I have amassed from my healing over the years would be enough to pay the *diyah*, but how can silver pay for the last breath leaving Faheem's red lips?

It is not enough. None of this would be enough, even if I were to confess – and who would believe me, a great healer of Kairouan, if I said that my desire for Faheem had made his heart pound until it broke? No, they would not believe me and my sin would go unpunished.

And so as the dawn call to prayer rings out across the city, I kneel to Allah and I make a vow. I will make amends for what I have done in my own way. I will serve Faheem's family until the day I die and still, in my own heart, it will not be enough. I am cold with certainty and purpose.

I claim no reward, I make no bargain, for who am I to bargain? I state only my decision, I do not ask that it is enough to expiate my sin.

My mother shakes her head. "Forever? You are only eighteen. You have your whole life before you. Don't be ridiculous."

I continue packing my clothes into a carved wooden chest. "As long as the girl needs me, I will serve her."

"But why?"

"Because I owe a debt."

My mother comes close to me, peers into my face. "What debt can you possibly have?"

I shake my head. "I cannot speak of it."

My mother begs my father to speak with me and he does, but our conversation goes round in circles, with him reminding me that as an eighteen-year old respected healer I surely owe no debt to anyone and what of my own life, my own future marriage?

To which I only reply that I cannot explain.

My mother tries weeping and for one brief moment I think my father is going to try his fists on me but at last they give up, agreeing between themselves that perhaps once I have helped this sick girl and she recovers (as surely she will in my care), I will put aside this nonsense and return home. To which I do not respond, only embrace my mother and father and ask for their blessing, which they reluctantly give.

The next morning I walk through the streets while the

dawn call to prayer echoes around me, the hood of my robe pulled up over my head. Behind me come two slaves, carrying the chest that holds all my possessions, such as they are. My silver I have already given to the poor, keeping only a few coins for myself.

Within a high wall sits the door into Safa's home. I do not call for a servant, I push the door with the palm of my hand and it opens onto the large courtyard of the house, a tinkling fountain surrounded by an elaborate tiled floor set all about with ornately carved and painted doors. This family has money. A servant carrying water pauses at the sight of me: an unexpected visitor at a too-early hour when half the family are still abed.

"Your mistress, Safa, sent for me," I tell her. "I am to see the daughter of the house, Djalila. Where is she?"

The girl hesitates but the fact that I have two slaves with me, my steady stare and the use of the family's names seems to convince her that I should be obeyed. "Her rooms are through there," she tells me. "Upstairs. The green door."

I dismiss the slaves, telling them to leave the chest in the courtyard. They begin to bid me farewell but I am already walking up the cold stone steps where I find a green-painted door. Again I do not wait to announce myself nor to be invited to enter. I open the door and approach the bed on which a girl lies sleeping.

I pause. The same red lips as her brother. Her hair as beautiful, but far longer. The same honey-gold skin. For several moments I stand over her and watch her breath rise and fall. At last I sit by her and turn over her wrist, let my fingertips rest on her pulse. Her eyes open in an instant.

"Who are you?" she demands, snatching her arm away

from me and sitting up, gathering her sleeping robes about her in a flurry of movement.

I sit still and look her over. Her arms are mostly bare and they are thinner than I have seen on street children or poorly-treated slaves. Her neck is scrawny, her cheekbones stick out too much, giving her the look of a hungry cat.

"Who are you and what are you doing in my room?" she yells at me.

"I am a healer," I say. "My name is Hela."

"I don't need a healer," she says. "Get out."

"You look ill," I say.

"My brother is dead!" she spits at me.

I swallow and steady my voice. It takes me a moment. "I know," I say. "I would have done anything to save him if I had known of his illness. Now I am here to help you."

"Did you know him?"

If she had asked me before he died I would have said yes. Yes, I knew him. I knew every tiny detail of his face, of his scent. He was all I thought of, of course I knew him. Now I know better. I shake my head. "I only saw him from a distance," I say. "You look like him," I cannot help adding. I do not say *your red lips*, but I think it.

Slowly she sits down on the other side of the bed from me. "He was my hero," she says. "My protector. Now I am all alone." Her eyes brim over with tears.

"You have your mother," I say. "Your father."

The tears stop abruptly. She sits very straight. "Get out," she says. "You know nothing of my life."

"It is not a happy life," I say.

She startles. "How do you know?"

I shrug. "You are half starved. You are grieving." I reach

out and touch her lightly on her bare arm and feel a wave of fear course through me. "You are afraid."

She is defiant. "Of what?"

I shake my head. "I don't know. Only you know who or what you are afraid of. I feel the fear, I do not know the cause. For now."

"And if you did know, you would save me?" she spits.

"Yes," I say.

She half-laughs, a bitter sound. "You wouldn't know where to start."

I stand up.

"Where are you going?"

"Downstairs."

"Don't leave me," she says and then looks down as though the words had escaped without her permission.

"I will be staying here," I tell her.

"For how long?" she challenges me.

"Forever, if I am needed," I say.

When I find Safa I tell her that I will be living in this house and serving her daughter until she is well. I do not tell her of my vow. One thing at a time, I think. When she exclaims at my plan I fix her with my most commanding stare and tell her that I will not leave this place until her daughter is well again. She, flustered, orders the servants that I am to be obeyed as though I were their mistress before blessing me and weeping. Unmoved, I leave her. Her blessings are meaningless, for she would be cursing me if she knew the truth. I return to Djalila's room.

"Get dressed," I tell her.

"I don't want to," she says, still muffled by her blankets.

"Rise," I say.

Something in my voice makes her struggle to a sitting position.

"I have told the slaves to bring hot water," I tell her. "Now you will wash."

"Leave the room," she says.

I shake my head.

"I will not undress in front of you," she says.

I stand, waiting.

Slowly, reluctantly, she strips off her sleeping robe and stands before me. She does not meet my eyes.

She is well formed enough, apart from her unnatural thinness. But her hair is lank and uncombed and she stands hunched, protecting herself from some unseen enemy. Near her shoulders and on the upper part of her thighs are bruises.

I kneel before my chest. I had the slaves bring it to the small room adjacent to Djalila's. I open the lid and have to take a deep breath. My mother has placed the red cup on top of the contents, perhaps believing that I would wish to have it and that I had left it behind by mistake. Carefully, I remove it and set it aside. I take out a small jar of ointment and smear it onto each bruise.

"Don't you want to know how I got them?" Djalila demands and I hear her voice tremble with the longing to tell me.

"You will tell me when you wish to," I say.

"I cannot," she says quickly.

"Then I will not ask you," I say. "You will tell me when you wish to."

She stands uncertain, then washes herself in silence, dresses in a robe too large for her.

"That does not fit you," I tell her. "I doubt it fitted you even when you were not this thin."

"I like my robes large," she says.

I look into her dark eyes and see fear there.

She says that she eats only in her own rooms but I make her follow me to the rooftop terrace, where a bright awning billows in the breeze and soft cushions are laid out for our comfort. Servants bring food and I watch while Djalila drinks tea but only picks at the freshly-cooked flatbreads until they are shredded into tiny crumbs, none of which have entered her mouth. I offer her a sorghum porridge and then boiled eggs but although she makes a great show of stirring the porridge and adding honey to it and then peeling the eggs, still none of the food is eaten. Her mother arrives while we are eating and fusses and frets until I ask her to leave us, which she does, looking back over her shoulder as though I am about to make a miracle happen.

We sit in silence for a while. I eat, for the food is good and I am hungry. My mind is mulling over what I have seen so far but as yet I have not understood why Djalila should be so thin, so fearful. I am drinking tea when I feel a wave of terror rise from her as a shadow falls over us. I look up.

"So you are the healer," says the man standing before us.

"I am," I say.

"I am Djalila's father," he says.

I stay silent but in my mind something settles into still certainty.

"I am grateful for your concern," he says. "But it will not be necessary for you to stay here. My daughter is well enough. It is her mother who thinks there is something wrong with her."

I do not look at him, only sip my tea. When I set down the cup I speak. "I will be here as long as she has need of me," I tell him.

"You will leave this house at once."

I stand in one fluid movement and step towards him. We are so close I can smell his breath. He towers over me but I do not break my gaze. "I will not," I tell him.

He raises his hand. "You will leave my house, you interfering bitch," he says.

"Do you wish me to explain to your wife why your daughter is like this?" I ask him. "Because I know."

His hand stops, mid-air. "You – " he begins but he does not finish. He looks at Djalila and then back at me. His hand drops to his side.

I gesture to Djalila without looking at her. "We will return to your room," I tell her.

She gets up quickly and scurries away from us both down the stairs. I look her father in the eyes. "If you wish to lay hands on some girl," I tell him, "go lie with a street woman who at least will be paid for her troubles. Do not touch your own daughter, you piece of filth."

He stands in silence as I leave the roof terrace and from that day onwards I barely see him. If we enter a room, he will quickly find some excuse why he must leave. In this way I am free to try and heal Djalila.

Day by day I entice her to eat. A little mouthful here, a scrap there. I make my way to the kitchen where I tell the cook to serve fat-streaked meat and dainty pastries soaked in honey and oil. Each mouthful she eats must be worth five. The cook has known Djalila since she was a child, she sets to with a will, making her favourite meals and adding richness to them. She serves them up in the tiny portions that are all Djalila will tolerate. She is my ally.

Slowly, slowly, Djalila recovers some flesh on her too-evident bones. I doubt she will ever attain rounded curves, but at least she does not look half-starved.

"You must marry," I tell her, when I see her smile for the first time in the three months that I have been her handmaiden.

Her face goes pale. "I do not want to marry!"

"You need to leave this house," I tell her. "You need to be the mistress of your own home or you will be forever looking over your shoulder, afraid your father is about to enter the room."

"He would not dare touch me now you are here," she tells me.

I shake my head. "Even if he never touches you again," I say, "why would you want to live under the same roof as him? If you had a good man you would be happy and free."

She looks afraid. "How would I know he would be a good man?"

"I will find one," I promise her. "But you need to leave this house."

I tell her mother that Djalila should be married and Safa, encouraged by Djalila's small improvements, calls on the matchmakers of the city to make it known that her daughter is ready for a husband. There is no shortage of offers for the family is well-off and Djalila is beautiful. Various suitors call on the family and with each of them I allow one fingertip to brush them as they pass me, I watch them as they meet with Djalila, who sits quiet and reserved in her still too-big robes.

Some are too passionate, too stricken with desire for her when they see her. Their lust is too great, they will frighten her, remind her of the suffering she has undergone. Others are too old, too much like her father and I can see for myself that she shrinks under their gaze. Some are very young and although a few fall in love with her I shake my head. Djalila needs a man who can be patient, who can woo her and bring her back to this world, who can bring her joy without demanding anything from her.

The man I choose for Djalila is named Ibrahim. He is the eldest son of one of the best carpet makers and traders in the city, a good and even match. Ibrahim himself is young, still in his twenties and although I can see his admiration for Djalila when he sets eyes on her, there is a softness, a sweetness to him that bodes well. He speaks to her of simple things – of the spring flowers opening up around the city and of his family, of his mother's fondness for cooking and his father's rounded belly and Djalila even smiles a little, she watches him when he leaves. When we are alone I nod and Djalila, still uncertain, nods back.

I visit his family's workshops without announcing myself, claiming that my unnamed mistress needs a new carpet for her rooms. Kairouan is renowned throughout the trading routes for its carpets. Ibrahim's family make some of the very best that the city can boast.

The workshop I visit is a chattering place, where the women who knot the carpets gossip amongst themselves. The looms sit before them, threaded in white. Bright balls of thread sit above their heads, trailing their colours down towards the women whose hands knot over and over again in quick movements. Each has a little knife to cut off a colour when she has no further use for it and reaches for another, barely glancing at the pattern as the carpets grow under their fingers, one thread, one knot, at a time. It is delicate work suited to women and those who work here are grateful to have secured such an occupation, prized work undertaken in a clean bright space. Not for them the dust of the potteries for women who paint the designs of pots, nor the close stench of the tanneries for the women whose families work in the leather trade. Their ears do not ring to the heavy beating of copper pots like the workers in Djalila's family business. Here the women can talk while they work and their surroundings are perfumed with roses, for Ibrahim's family believe in scenting the air so that their sought-after carpets will perfume the houses of their customers. I run my hand over the fine wares, feigning interest in their patterns while I watch Ibrahim's family members as they go about their business. His father relies on his children's labour now, contenting himself with sitting in a corner of the workshop, sipping mint tea and jovially teasing them.

"Look at your youngest brother, Ibrahim, there's a way to sell a carpet to a woman, all sweet words and sidelong glances!"

Ibrahim laughs out loud. "He's nothing but a scoundrel and you'd better find him a wife, Father, before one of those ladies claims him for her own!"

Ibrahim's two sisters, as yet unmarried, look up from their work. They are elevated above the women who weave, for each has been taught how to design carpets and they sit musing over future creations, adding a swirl here or a flower there to satisfy their demanding eyes.

They giggle at the exchange and call to a servant to go and buy sweets from a nearby stall. "We can't be working on empty bellies!"

"You work on honey, nuts and pastries," reprimands their father with a grin. "And then turn your noses up at good home cooked food."

"Honey makes the carpets prettier," returns the elder daughter with a smirk, passing a few sweetmeats to the working women.

Something loosens inside me. These are good people. They enjoy life and they relish one another's company. I am changing Djalila's life for the better. She will grow healthy in my care and perhaps her happiness will atone a little for Faheem's lost life. Perhaps she will be happy with a kind and gentle husband and slowly, slowly, I will be set free of the guilt that weighs me down so greatly that when I think of it I can barely lift one foot in front of the other.

Djalila's father catches me on the stairs.

"I forbid this marriage," he hisses at me.

"On what grounds?" I ask him.

He does not answer.

"If you wish to forbid the marriage," I say, "you had better announce your reasons for it before the whole family. And wait for me to have my say."

He stands silently in the shadows as I walk away and no more is said.

Meanwhile her mother is delighted and in no time all manner of fine silks are flowing into the house and Djalila, for once, must wear robes that are more suited to her slender form. When I see her dressed in a blue that rivals the sea, her long dark hair brushed loose as she tries on the golden headdress she will wear, there is a moment when I have to look away from her beauty, which reminds me too much of Faheem.

She is resplendent on her wedding day. The bridal headdress shines atop her magnificent black hair, her large dark eyes are a little wary but also filled with something resembling hope. Her father's face is a thundercloud but I curse him in my mind. The ceremony begins and she looks down in modesty but a little flush of colour rises on her cheeks and I follow her to Ibrahim's new home with relief. His parents have other sons and their families who live with them and so he has set up a home of his own close by to them where his bride will reign as mistress all alone, un-subjected to her in-laws, a rare freedom. I have chosen well.

The house is large. The courtyard is filled with flowers, a fountain splashes. A tree brings added shade within the cool of the tiled space. Above our heads stretch two more floors, glimpsed by balconies and carved plasterwork. The doors are thick wood, painted and carved to a high standard. This is a wealthy house, equal to or better than Djalila's old home. She has done well to secure such a husband.

A woman awaits us, large-breasted, wide-hipped, an air of authority. Slaves stand behind her, other servants peek at us from the entrance to the kitchen.

"I am Hayfa," she tells Djalila. "Your cook, mistress."

Djalila says nothing.

"I am Hela," I tell Hayfa. "I am your mistress' handmaiden and I will command in her place. My mistress does not like to be troubled with household matters."

I can see Hayfa wants to contest this statement. Who has ever heard of a handmaiden commanding in her mistress' place, unless that mistress is old or ill? She frowns but I keep my eyes on her and after a moment she drops her gaze.

"Very well," she mutters. "As my mistress desires."

"How many servants are there?" I ask.

"Four," she says. "And the slaves, of course." Clearly she does not think slaves are worth counting.

I nod. "Where are my mistress' rooms?" I ask.

Hayfa glances warily at Djalila, who has stood in silence throughout all of this. "I will take you," she says.

The servants and slaves watch us as we make our way up the stairs, no doubt wondering what their new mistress is like, sizing me up and speculating on my excessive power.

There are two rooms for Djalila, a bedroom and a larger room in which she may spend her days if she wishes for privacy. I hope that I will be able to entice her out of them. They are well appointed, there is nothing missing that a woman could wish for. Beautiful carpets and hangings, of course, as one might expect. The scent of roses throughout the house. Great carved chests of sweet-smelling wood await our possessions, which the slaves are now carrying up to us.

Hayfa shows us other parts of the house. There is a study where Ibrahim can keep track of his wares and sales, where the precious paper patterns are stored for safekeeping. On the shelves there are many books, perhaps more than twenty, great tomes made with skill.

"Your master reads?" I ask Hayfa. I am surprised. The richer merchants of the city can read well enough and certainly they know their numbers, to manage their accounts and supplies, but I know of none that read for pleasure.

"He wanted to be a scholar," says Hayfa. "But his father commanded he should take over the carpet business, being the eldest son. Still, he insisted on having books in his home." She looks at them with a mixture of pride and uneasiness, as though they are wild animals that might bite her. "He has scholars from the university to eat with him sometimes," she adds, her tone suggesting that this is a very odd pastime but that she is aware that it somehow makes her master important. "They talk all night."

I lift one down from the shelf.

"Don't touch them!" says Hayfa. "Master's orders are that no-one is to touch them."

I open the book. "*The Book of Fixed Stars*," I read. "It speaks of astronomy, the study of the heavens."

Hayfa stares at me, dumbfounded. "You can read?"

I nod, still turning the pages. I am impressed that Ibrahim has continued his interest in such things despite his father's attempts to turn him to a different path.

After this exchange I see that Hayfa treats me with greater respect although she never does get over her wariness of me. I do not gossip with her, I am no ordinary servant, I have too much power for her to relax in my company. She keeps to her realm and I keep to mine: she does as I tell her but speaks about me behind my back to the other servants as though I am some strange creature.

Djalila is shaking.

"He is a gentle man," I repeat. I have been saying this all day. "He will be kind to you," I add, hoping that this is true. "He will not force you. You must trust me."

She says nothing.

I apply rose perfume to her skin, brush out her long hair, undress her and place the bedcovers around her.

There is a soft knock at the door and Djalila clutches at me, her eyes wide.

"I have to go now," I say, trying to prise her fingers off my arm.

"Don't leave me," she whispers and I feel pity for her but what can I do? I cannot tell Ibrahim her history, nor can I refuse him entrance to his bride's bedchamber on their wedding night. As it is I have arranged for there not to be a crowd gathered about the place, cheering and making lewd comments. I pull my arm away and stand up, open the door to Ibrahim.

"My mistress is a little shy," I murmur to him. "You will be patient with her, master?"

He smiles as though I am a fussing old woman. "You may leave us now, Hela," he says and I bow my head and leave the room.

I wait and I listen. I hear Ibrahim speaking softly with her. I cannot make out what he is saying, yet he sounds very tender. There is little response from Djalila, I strain to hear her voice but am not sure she is answering him. I kneel and pray to Allah for this night to be successful, for Djalila to see that all can be well in the bedchamber.

Instead I hear a few little cries of fear and pain before there is silence and then Ibrahim's footsteps warn me to hide myself. I see him leave her room, his brow furrowed, walking swiftly to his own rooms.

Inside Djalila weeps.

"Did he…" I ask.

She shakes her head.

"He tried?"

She nods.

My shoulders slump. "He was gentle?" I ask.

She nods, miserable.

I sigh. "Then it will get better," I say firmly, though I am doubtful. "You will grow accustomed to him, he is gentle as I promised, he will not force you. You must only grow your courage a little, Djalila."

She sobs and I have to spend half the night comforting her. At breakfast Ibrahim is kind, he speaks softly with her, he offers her warm bread with honey and she takes it from him and tries to smile. I see his face lighten a little, no doubt he thinks the matter will soon be resolved.

But the nights pass and the shadows under my eyes grow dark from listening to one failed attempt after another and every night I praise Allah that Ibrahim has not forced himself upon her, as by now many men would have done. I beg for Ibrahim to have a little more patience. Meanwhile I try to build up Djalila's confidence and happiness in her new home.

I try to tempt her out into the streets. She is a married woman now, not a child, she need not cower in her rooms. Kairouan is a great city, a rich city. Sitting on the trading routes, it is home to people from across the Maghreb, for one day or a lifetime. I try to entice her out on the great market days, when thousands of people come from far and wide to buy and sell. I take her through the souks and suggest she might want to buy fine cloth to have robes made, sweetmeats, jewellery. Ibrahim is a generous husband, she can buy whatever she wishes for. But the jostling of the crowds, the blood running in the streets from the hundreds of animals slaughtered, the noise and smells make her shudder and beg to return to our peaceful courtyard, to the safety of her rooms.

I take her into the quieter countryside surrounding the city, where she can see the rich fields swaying with grain, the silvered leaves of ancient olive trees, the fat sheep whose wool supplies her husband with the means to weave the finest carpets of Kairouan. We watch as, before dawn, pickers bend to pluck rose petals before the heat takes their fragrance. They will make the rose oil that perfumes the women of the city and makes men tremble with desire. I try their wares and buy them for the house and workshop, but Djalila says the smell is too much and she turns away, stares at the rising sun's pale rays and the mists floating in the valleys.

We visit the reservoirs outside the city walls that bring water to the city. These great pools protect us from droughts and allow the fine households of the city to have playing fountains even in the great heat of summer. The pools are a deep green colour, dark as the depths of the water. Ibrahim tries to take Djalila there but she does not like the chatter and noise around her, the attention of other people. So I take her there during the daytimes when only street children play near them, splashing each other and laughing. She watches them as though she would like to join them and once or twice I splash her on purpose, to see if I can make her laugh, if she will forget herself and become the child she left behind but she cannot, she only shrinks from me and begs me not to do it again and so I desist and we sit in silence until I take her home again.

At last I think that perhaps she could gain confidence through faith, for some women find great solace in it. Kairouan is a holy city. The water from the Bi'r Barouta well is holy, for a river supposedly flows between here and Mecca. If you drink enough of it you are exempted from a visit to Mecca, so I take Djalila to the well, that she can drink and feel blessed. We stand by the blindfolded camel who trudges round and round to pull up the water. We drink the fresh cold water from little cups and I tell Djalila that she is a lucky woman to live in such a holy place. She sips from the cup and nods, silent and meek as a cowed child. I take her to pray at the towering mosque with its myriad ancient columns, but she is uncomfortable with crowds and prefers to pray in her own rooms. I do not know what she asks Allah for, what desires she has, for even to me she is closed.

I try to encourage her in meeting other young wives with whom she might pass the time. But on the few occasions when such a woman seems friendly, a neighbour, the wife of a fellow tradesman, Djalila shrinks from them, stays silent as though displeased and I see them falter in their speech, their smiles fade and they do not invite her back to their homes, do not return to visit ours.

At last I speak with her. "Ibrahim is a kind man," I tell her. "But the moon has waned twice since you were married and he will lose patience. You must succumb to him, you must be his wife in more than name, Djalila, or he may force himself upon you or even put you aside."

Her eyes well up.

"I know you are scared," I say to her. "I will ask him not to visit you often. But if you can give him some children you will secure your place as his wife and then he might even be persuaded to go elsewhere for his pleasures. Please, Djalila."

"Watch over me," she begs.

I gape at her. "I cannot watch you while you are with your husband," I say.

"I need you there," she says. "I feel safe when you are by my side."

I stand in the shadows where I will not be seen. My heart beats hard for I will be surely be turned out if Ibrahim catches me and yet Djalila asks this service of me and so I must obey, to try and secure her happiness. I try not to look but still I catch glimpses, of Ibrahim's body as he strips off his robes and his limbs intertwine with hers.

I cannot fault his patience. He offers gentle caresses and soft words, he uses his lips to touch her skin and his hands smooth her dark hair where it lies tumbled on the pillow. When he enters her he is not rough and his arms hold her with tenderness, though her hands stay clenched throughout and her eyes stay fixed on me over Ibrahim's muscled shoulders.

And so Ibrahim leaves her room with a smile rather than a frown, though it is I who has to hold her while she cries afterwards.

"You might come to enjoy it," I suggest, thinking of his soft words, his lips on her skin. But she only shakes her head in misery.

The next day Ibrahim gives her a magnificent necklace and places it smilingly about her neck, but she hides her face.

I follow him as he goes to his rooms. "I am sorry my mistress is not more willing," I say. "She is very timid. I ask on her behalf that you do not visit her too often, but I will tell you the days when she is most likely to conceive a child."

He is not best pleased, this I can see. But perhaps he

believes that the matter will improve over time. "Very well," he says, his good humour lost as he turns away.

And so his visits to her rooms lessen and I need only watch their twisting shapes in the flickering light of lanterns for a few days in each month, sometimes casting my eyes down, sometimes drawn helplessly to watch. Djalila still shrinks from his touch but at least she does what is expected of her.

She has other duties. Ibrahim is firm on few things, but on this he is certain. "Your place is by my side when we entertain guests," he tells Djalila. "As my mother sits by my father's side. You must dress well, you must smile. A trader who buys carpets must think of luxury when he buys from us, of beauty and perfume, of comfort and generosity. Our carpets are not just the knots that make them but the reputation that goes before them."

And so Djalila dresses with care and descends to entertain guests. She twitches beforehand, she trembles but I stand in the room where she can see me and she learns to do this one thing well. She speaks little but she smiles and she stays by Ibrahim's side, no matter how late the evening wears on, no matter how dull the talk. Guests to the house notice her beauty. Her silence they take for the appropriate demureness of a woman from a good family and they praise her for it. They buy in large quantities from Ibrahim because of the quality of his hospitality and in turn Ibrahim smiles on Djalila, comforted that in this duty, at least, his wife is accomplished and a credit to him. On the nights when Ibrahim does not need to entertain traders he entertains his own choice of guests, philosophers and men of the law, holy men and they talk for many hours. On these nights Djalila is excused early and it is only I who stand in the shadows or squat outside the door, the better to learn from these men. The months pass and at last, at last, Djalila retches and turns pale. I place my hand on her and feel a new life beginning.

Ibrahim

ALL NIGHT I PACE WHILE the midwife attends to Djalila. Below, in the courtyard, Ibrahim matches my paces, step for step. He, perhaps, longs for a boy: I pray only that no harm comes to Djalila. Every cry she makes pierces me and I berate the midwife more than once.

"Give her something for the pain!" I shout at her at last, when Djalila's screams grow so loud that they rock the household.

The midwife is an old hag who has done her work for a great deal longer than I have been alive and she almost laughs at me.

"She is well enough," she says complacently. "The pain is normal."

"Make her stop screaming," I say through gritted teeth.

"You used to be a healer," she says. "You give her something."

I shake my head. "I do not use my skills," I say.

"Why not?" she asks, her eyes sharp and bright on me.

"Mind your own business," I tell her. "Make her stop screaming."

"She'll stop when the baby comes," she says.

I curse her and walk away, to another room, but Djalila

shrieks for me not to leave her and so, reluctantly, I return to her side, to feel wave after wave of fear, Djalila's pain coursing through me so strongly that I nearly scream myself.

Time passes so slowly that I think there must be some trick being played on me. Surely the sun should rise, where is the dawn call to prayer? And still the night goes on.

At last Djalila's screams change and the midwife bestirs herself.

"The baby will come now," she says with certainty and she makes Djalila kneel on the bed.

When the tiny slippery body emerges the midwife barely holds it before passing it to me, wrapped in a cloth. I hold the mewling, wriggling, still-wet body in my hands and stare down at it.

"Boy or girl?" asks the midwife.

I pull the cloth a little to one side. "Girl," I say.

"Ah well, she is alive at least and has a strong cry," sniffs the midwife. "It will be a boy next time, if Allah wills it."

I offer the baby to Djalila but she is too weary. She holds the baby for only a moment and then passes her back to me and closes her eyes.

"Keep a watch on her," says the midwife. "Any sign of a fever, send for me. And make the baby suckle."

"How?" I ask but she is already gone.

Ibrahim stands outside the door, hovering tentatively. I give him the baby and he holds her as though she might break. He gazes down on the little body in delight.

"What will you name her?" I ask.

"Zaynab," he says, as though he has had this name ready for a long time. "Flower of the desert. She is a little flower." His voice is unsteady with tenderness.

I cannot help smiling at him and he returns the smile.

"I am sorry she is not a son," I offer politely.

He shrugs. "It is only the first child," he says, cheerful with relief. "There will be more and Allah will grant us a son."

I nod and take back Zaynab. Her fists ball up and she wails.

"I think she needs feeding," I say helplessly.

Ibrahim nods and backs away, leaving me alone with the baby and the sleeping Djalila.

Awkwardly I try to make the baby suckle but she does not seem to understand what to do. Gently I wake Djalila to help me, although since neither of us know how to encourage her, there is not much improvement.

"I am too tired," says Djalila, her eyes closing again.

She sleeps for a long time, during which the baby sleeps a little but mostly wails. When I try to wake Djalila again, her skin feels hot and in a panic I send a slave running for the midwife.

The woman shakes her head when she sees the sweat forming on Djalila's skin. "You had better find a wet-nurse for the child," she says bluntly.

"And Djalila? What should we do for her?"

She shakes her head. "Once there's a fever they rarely recover," she says.

I feel a coldness sink into me. "I cannot lose another," I say in a whisper. "I swore."

"What did you say?" says the old woman.

"Nothing," I say.

I send a servant to find a wet nurse for Zaynab and leave her in the arms of the midwife, who sits by Djalila's panting, shaking side. I make my way to my room and kneel down to open the chest I have rarely opened since I first went to serve Djalila's family. Slowly I lift the lid and remove the cloth that covers the contents.

The red cup lies there, its dull surface seeming like something broken or dead. I touch it, wondering if it still has powers. I feel nothing.

I set to work. I mix herbs to cool a fever, herbs to strengthen, herbs to make a womb healthy. I am so frantic I forget half of what I know. Even while I choose one herb and then another I know that I do not believe that any of the ingredients I am using will offer a cure: I know that what I truly believe is that the cure will come from the cup itself, that it hardly matters what I put into it. While I mix the medicine I pour all of my prayers into it, my hope that it will cure Djalila, that she will not die. If she dies then I will have failed in serving her, I will be guilty once more of allowing harm to come to Faheem's family.

I am not gentle with Djalila. She coughs and splutters and moans but I slip my fingers between her teeth and hold her mouth open as though she were an animal, pouring the liquid down her throat while a good portion of it dribbles down her sweating chin and stains her blankets. The midwife watches me with interest.

"I thought you said you did not use your skills," she says.

"Be quiet," I tell her. "Look after the child, you've already half-killed her mother."

"Not my fault," she tells me. "I told you, once the fever starts a woman is as good as dead, whatever you're giving her."

I don't answer her. I sit on Djalila's bed, wiping the sweat off her clammy skin. I am so focused on her that I am only dimly conscious of a wet-nurse arriving, a plump woman who has the baby suckling in moments. The silence, after her constant cries, should be a relief but all it means is that I can hear Djalila's panting breath more loudly.

I had thought the previous night long, but the day passes in a haze of exhaustion. Again and again I feel my head jerk upright. Again and again I force the brew I have made down Djalila and when the distant calls to prayer can be heard I kneel to beg for help and think that I will fall asleep even as I touch my head to the ground. By nightfall the wet-nurse has been comfortably installed in the house and the midwife, shaking her head, has left us.

I sleep. I cannot stay awake. My body slumps by Djalila's side, the cup still in my hand, the last dregs of the drink leaking onto the cold floor. I dream of Faheem, see his red lips and hear a baby crying, see the heaving bodies of Ibrahim and Djalila and her red-rimmed eyes afterwards. When I awake there is a thin pale light and my legs have lost all feeling. I am stiff with cold and for a moment I forget why I am here and what I have been doing. The room is silent and wearily I turn my head to look at Djalila, expecting her to be lifeless, for I cannot hear her panting.

Her skin is pale but no longer clammy. She is asleep, not dead. I have to touch her breast and feel her heartbeat before I am certain and I lift the sheets to see if there is blood but there is only a little. She is not dead, nor even dying.

I pick up the cup and walk slowly back to my own room. Along the way I catch sight of a slave girl.

"Take food and clean water for bathing to your mistress," I tell her. "Tell the master she is safe. And make sure the wet-nurse is well fed."

"Praise be to Allah," says the girl. "Shall I bring you food and water also?"

"I am going to sleep," I tell her.

I sleep for a day and a night and a day again. When I awake I wash the cup before I wash myself, then I wrap it in a soft cloth and lock it away again. I wash the stink of sweat and fear from my body and dress before descending to eat.

"Praise be to Allah, Djalila has recovered," says Ibrahim. "And I gather it was down to your care."

I shake my head. I do not want to talk about the red cup nor what was in it. "I did nothing," I say.

"The midwife said otherwise," says Ibrahim earnestly. "And I thank you for what you did, whatever it was. Djalila will be able to bear more children, thanks to you."

"No!" I say loudly and Ibrahim looks shocked at my outburst.

"No what?" he asks.

"She is not to have another child," I tell him. "Not soon, not ever."

"But…" he begins.

"No," I tell him and my voice is cold. "She must not have another child. I saved her once, I cannot do it again."

Ibrahim looks at me in disbelief. "What do you

suggest?" he asks. "Another wife to share my bed and bring me sons?"

I shake my head. "Djalila would be crushed," I tell him.

"So what do you suggest?" he asks me.

"Take me," I say and I know as I say them that these words have been waiting all this time in my mouth, that as the months have passed I have been wooed by Ibrahim without either of us knowing it. That something in me has taken his learning, his soft words and the sight of his flesh pressed against Djalila's and fashioned them into my own desire. "Take me."

He refuses at first. Whether out of repugnance for me or love for Djalila, I do not know. But time goes by and I see him watching me. I see him look my way when Djalila goes to her bedchamber and I know he can only wait so long before his desires bring him to me.

I visit baby Zaynab in her nursery from time to time. She learns to crawl, exploring the world around her, her chubby hands grasping at whatever she can reach, wondering at what she finds. Her black hair fuzzes around her face, framing huge dark eyes and honey skin, along with tiny red lips, which close around anything she can get into her mouth before her wetnurse stops her. She beams when she sees anyone, expecting only love.

I dare not love her. I fear all my passions, how they grow out of nothing into such desires that they threaten those around me. And so when I wish to clasp her in my arms and stroke her soft black curls, when I want to hide my face behind my hands and then playfully show myself to her again to make her laugh I do not. Instead I retreat, turn my face away when she smiles at me and return to Djalila's rooms. Ibrahim does not spend much time with Zaynab, perhaps he thinks it is a woman's task, perhaps she reminds him of the sons he will not have. Djalila, despite my urgings, does not visit Zaynab much. Perhaps she reminds her of her own shortcomings as a wife. And so Zaynab grows, clutching at chests and beds until she takes her own unsteady steps surrounded only by servants, unaided by those people who should offer her love, her own parents and myself, each of us too tightly wrapped in our own fears and desires.

More than a year passes before a night comes when the heat is too great for anyone in the city to sleep. Djalila tosses and turns in the room next to me and I hear Zaynab wail more than once, her nursemaid shushing her with some old lullaby and a fan. The maids splash one another with water as darkness falls and then retreat to their own room, giggling between themselves at the names of this boy or that, their empty imaginations running riot.

I hear Ibrahim's footsteps come up the stairs and pause, first outside Djalila's room and then outside of mine. I hold my breath for a moment and hear the thudding of my heart before his footsteps turn away. I hear him climb the stairs to the roof terrace, perhaps the only place where the night air might bring the hope of coolness.

I rise, then, and follow the echo of his steps. When

I reach the rooftop he is standing with his hands on the perimeter wall, looking out over the night city. Here and there lanterns flicker, above us stars cover the sky in a pale glow.

"I have treated her with kindness," he says without turning.

"Yes," I say.

"I have not forced myself upon her."

"No," I say.

"I have made her mistress of her own home and all has been done to her satisfaction, to her command. She has but to say the word and she is obeyed. She has everything a woman may desire."

"Yes," I say.

"But she is not happy. She will not lie with me of her own desire. I have only one child by her and now no hope of any others."

"No," I say.

He is silent for a moment and far away we hear carts rattling through the streets, the clip-clop of hooves going by in the alleyways outside, traders readying themselves for the dawn.

"Have I done something wrong?" he asks.

"No," I say.

"I need more than Yes and No," he says. "I need to know what is wrong."

"She is damaged," I tell him.

"By what?"

"Things that happened to her as a child," I say. "I cannot tell you of them."

"And she will never recover, is that it? I chose a wife

who had a hidden flaw in her, one that I could not see beneath her beauty and now there is no way to heal her?"

"If I knew a way I would do it," I say.

He is silent again and I step forward, take up a place beside him, look out at what he can see, the dark rooftops and the stars above.

"I am at fault," I say and the words come fast because it is a relief to me not to hold them in. "I chose you as her husband."

"What?"

"She had many suitors. I chose you."

"Who were you to choose?"

"Her handmaiden," I say. "Her companion. I made her as well as I could and I thought she should marry. I thought if she found a kind man, a man who would help her to be happy, if she had a house of her own and could be its mistress, that it would heal her."

"Why me?"

"You were a good man," I say. "I saw it in you. I – I felt it in you. When I met you I felt your kindness, your patience. She would not have to live with elder members of a family, she could have the freedom of being her own mistress at once. And – and you did not just lust after her, you cared for her."

"How do you know?"

"I saw it in your eyes," I say. "And the day of the gift giving. You brought all the traditional things – the sheep, the fruits, the jewellery – but you brought her flowers as well, the ones she wore in her hair the first time you ever saw her. And so I knew you had thought of her."

He shrugs. "I thought we would be happy together," he says. "Now it seems that will never be possible."

"It is my fault," I say. "I have made you miserable even though I meant for the two of you to be happy."

"Why do you serve her?" he asks.

"I hurt her family a long time ago," I say. "I swore to serve them until I die."

He shakes his head. "That sound like a child's promise."

"Perhaps it was," I say. "But I made a vow and I will keep it."

"And what do you propose I do now?" he asks.

I swallow and keep my eyes on the stars. "Lie with me," I half-whisper into the darkness.

"And Djalila?"

"She will not know," I say. "I will never tell her."

"And in this way you seek to make us both happy?"

"Yes," I say.

"And will you be happy?" he asks.

Yes, I think. *Yes.* "I will be content," I say and even as I speak his arms are around me.

I keep my promise. Djalila may wonder a little at Ibrahim's no longer coming to her rooms, but the relief she feels stops her from enquiring further. She grows a little happier. She still stays mostly in her own rooms but she allows me to open up the shutters more often, she lets the sun touch her skin, sometimes she will even watch people go by outside her windows. She sends me to buy songbirds in the souk and they fill her rooms with a semblance of life that has been missing until now, their chirps and bright feathers even make her smile a little. By day I manage the household while Ibrahim is in the workshops, Zaynab toddles about the courtyard garden and Djalila, perhaps, begins to heal a little. Once or twice a month she may even call for Zaynab and spend a little time with her, though she is awkward in the child's presence, unable to think what to say or do. I try to encourage her, buying little sweets for her to give the child or suggesting that she encourages Zaynab to play with the birds but Djalila is so stilted in making such offers that Zaynab senses her discomfort and grows awkward herself, shrinking away from possible caresses and eventually retreating behind her nursemaid's legs. Yet when Ibrahim's sisters come they squeeze her and ignore her shrieks, poking her till she giggles, stuffing her mouth with dripping honey cakes and she submits to their round-bellied, double-chinned embraces, feigning a desire to escape but returning to them over and over again as she runs about the house.

I visit Zaynab in her nursery sometimes. The nursemaid I have chosen for her, Myriam, is a plump young woman, full of chatter, the opposite of Djalila and indeed myself. She feeds Zaynab plentifully, she occasionally hugs her for no reason, she berates her for many small reasons, loudly and without malice so that Zaynab pays little attention. She is almost four now, a real little girl rather than a waddling baby. Her hair is dark and curly, her lips are red, her skin is honeyed perfection. She runs about the house, noisy and curious. Often I will see her dark eyes peeping from behind a hanging or a door and I try to smile at her but she flits away, frightened. I know the servants tell tales about me, casting me as the all-powerful handmaiden to their unstable mistress.

By night I make my way to the rooftop. I hold Ibrahim to me and revel in a man's desire, feel his lips on my skin and look up into the thousand thousand stars that shine above me. On moonlit nights I watch the play of our limbs as our skins shine in the darkness and I feel love begin to grow in me. I attempt to keep it at bay. I keep my mind only on my own pleasure, I do not think how to please him, I hold back from caressing him when he lies spent by my side. I do not speak, I do not whisper such words as come to mind when we are together. I do not let him speak either, for I am afraid of what he would say and of my own response. I do not allow his lips to touch mine, for to kiss seems too close to love. Each day I drink the herbs that will stop a child from growing in my womb, even though it tastes bitter to me.

But I am not able to hold back my feelings. A year comes and goes and then another. And I find myself thinking of Ibrahim, I find myself waiting for his return from the workshops. I order meals that will please him. I wear robes that will be soft on his hands when he undresses me. I smooth my skin with oils for his pleasure. The night comes when his lips brush against mine and I do not turn my face away. And I grow afraid. I drink the bitter herbs and they taste sweet in my mouth. I am afraid of what the cup may do, how it might turn the bitterness to something else and allow a child to grow because I wish for it even while I drink the herbs that guard against it. I stop using the cup for myself but even when I use another cup, still I wonder if my own desires will turn against me.

"Marry me," says Ibrahim one night as the stars begin to shine above us.

Something in me twists. In one moment I think of marriage to Ibrahim. Of happiness, of a child perhaps. Of being free to love. To love Ibrahim, to love Zaynab. But I see Djalila's face, her red lips.

"I cannot," I say.

"Do not be so hasty," he says. "Think of it again."

I bow my head in silence.

I do not sleep that night. Ibrahim sleeps and I lie by his side and watch him. I think of my vow and wonder whether I have atoned sufficiently. After all, I think, I rescued Djalila from her father. She has the kindest of husbands, a child, a good household. What would change in her life? Better that I be her co-wife than who-knows-who, some younger, more beautiful woman to break her heart. Perhaps we could grow closer, be as sisters. The sky grows pale as dawn approaches and my heart lightens. I think that perhaps this offer from Ibrahim is a sign from Allah, an acknowledgement that I have tried to fulfill my vow and that I am released from its bonds. I look down at Ibrahim and smile. When he wakes I will tell him that I will be his wife.

Screams suddenly echo throughout the house, followed by running footsteps from every part of the building and then Hayfa's voice overlays the screams with shouts for help. She calls my name.

"Hela! *Hela*!"

I run down the stairs, half-dressed, my robes in disarray, my hair tumbling about my shoulders, not yet bound up for the day. In the house's courtyard garden are gathered all the servants and slaves, so that I cannot see what is going on but as I approach Hayfa shoves them away.

"Get out of the way. Let her through!"

The youngest member of Hayfa's team, a slave boy, is hurt. He is barely ten, a scrawny dark-skinned thing my father would have turned his nose up at, but lively enough. He runs errands for Hayfa in the souk, taking bread to the ovens or carrying heavy loads home for her through the twisting turning paths of the souk. Now he lies just inside the courtyard's door, one leg at an impossible angle, blood seeping from it, bruises already forming. I catch a glimpse of white bone against his black skin, more sickening for the contrast.

"What happened?" I ask.

"We were buying pastries. A cart crushed him. The donkey was frightened by something, it went careering into him. His body was flung against a wall so hard he did not reply when I spoke to him," says Hayfa, her face pale. "The wheel trapped his leg under it."

I look down at the boy. Even as I do so he closes his eyes and his whole body shakes, only the whites of his eyes showing as his mouth opens and saliva flows down his chin. One of the servant girls cries out that he is cursed and Hayfa slaps her so hard she falls to the ground. The others draw back. At the back of the group I catch a glimpse of Ibrahim and Djalila, drawn by the commotion.

"Help him," says Hayfa to me.

"I cannot," I say.

She looks at me as though I have spat in her face. "I said help him," she tells me. "He is losing his wits and his leg is broken. How can you stand there and do nothing when you have healing skills?"

"What do you know of what I can do?" I ask.

"You saved the mistress," says Hayfa.

"That was luck," I say.

"It was the red cup," says Hayfa with stubborn certainty.

I feel a thud in my belly as though she has punched me. "What did you say?" I ask.

The slave boy shakes under our hands.

"I asked about you around Kairouan," says Hayfa. "You were the great healer. You used a magical red cup."

I kneel down. "Put your hands here," I tell her. "Do not let his thigh move."

"You – "

"Do it," I say and she does what I tell her to do.

Bone grates on bone and one of the servant girls faints behind us. My eyes are closed but I feel the bone as it turns, meets its rightful place and I grip his leg and tell the servants to bring cloths, so that I can wrap it tightly. I use splints to hold the leg in place and tell Hayfa that I have done all I can.

"He must drink from the cup," she says.

"I no longer use it," I say.

"He must drink from it," she insists.

I make a meaningless drink, something that will bring strength and I give it to Hayfa. "Hold it to his lips," I say. I know that her desire to help him, transmitted through the cup, will do more than whatever I have mixed together.

She holds it as though it is a sacred vessel and ensures he drinks every drop.

"If you want him to live he will have to stay in your kitchen without moving for more than two months," I say. "He will not be able to run errands for you."

"He never did much anyway," she scoffs, her relief masked as disdain. "I daresay I can keep an eye on him."

"He will always limp," I warn her.

"What's a limp?" she says, defensive. "Half of Kairouan limps with one malady or another."

I stand up and walk away, past Djalila. Ibrahim follows me back to the rooftop. When we reach the terrace I turn to him.

"I cannot," I say.

"Why?"

I think of my dawn smile, of my foolish belief that I was released from my vow. It was not a release, it was a test and I failed it. The slave boy's accident is my warning. I have not been faithful to the vow I made.

I say what I should have said long ago. "I cannot marry you, Ibrahim. And I can no longer lie with you."

"If you cannot and Djalila will not," he says, and I can hear hurt as well as a growing anger in his voice, "then what do you suggest?"

"Take another wife," I say quickly, before I can unsay the words.

"You said before that Djalila – "

"Leave her to me," I say.

"Very well," he says, looking down at the ground. "I will find another wife. And may Allah help me choose better than I did the first time."

"I will choose a wife for you," I say.

"No," he says.

"A young wife," I say, words tumbling from me. "A healthy wife, a wife who will be good to you, kind to Zaynab. Who will not be afraid of Djalila's ways."

"If such a woman exists," he snorts and turns away.

I stand alone on the rooftop and hold my robes closer against a chill only I can feel. How will it be to have another woman here, a woman who will share Ibrahim's bed? How will I bear it? How will Djalila react? I shake my head. I cannot ask myself such questions. I have hurt too many lives already. I have been warned. I must try harder. I will find a good woman to heal this household.

Imen

I TOUCH IMEN MORE THAN ONCE to be certain, doubting myself. I am so used to the beats of Ibrahim's frustration and my own wretched guilt, to Zaynab's pitiful cravings for a love that is not given, to the pulse of Djalila's endless secret fears, that to touch someone and feel only happiness, only innocent joy in life, is startling to me. I return to her again and again, drawn to feel her gentleness. I pull up the hood of a heavy robe over my face and walk the streets of the souk to find her and when I do I let one finger brush against her and find once again her light heartbeats, bright and full of certainty in the goodness of her life. When I walk on I hope that perhaps her light will enter my darkness and take away the bitterness within me.

She is not from a very great family but they are good people, no-one can say anything against them when I listen for gossip. Ibrahim's sisters beam when I murmur to them of a possible match.

Ibrahim is wary, as well he might be. He does not trust me. "I must see her for myself," he says.

I watch him leave the house for a visit to her father's

house and want to call him back, want to lean from the rooftop that was our secret place and cry out his name, but I bite my lips and clench my fists instead and know that I must not.

He cannot help smiling at the thought of her when he tells me that he has asked for her hand. He tries to hide it from me but I can see that her sweet face and gentle demeanour have awakened hope in him. I lower my eyes and murmur that I am glad, that I will see to it that all will be done to please her in this house.

"I must tell Djalila," he says.

"No," I say too quickly. "I will do it."

He shakes his head, stubborn in his knowledge of what is right. "No," he says. "It must come from me."

There is silence from her room when he emerges and I pause for a moment as I pass him. "Did she cry?" I ask.

He shakes his head and walks away.

I take a breath and then enter.

Djalila sits with a bird in her hand. It pecks lightly at the grain she holds for it and she gazes at it as though it is all she can see.

"Did he tell you?" she asks without looking at me. "Or did you already know?"

"There is no shame," I say. "You are his first wife and you have given him a child."

"A girl," she says.

"A healthy child," I say. "And you nearly died in doing so. The new wife will bear more children but she will never be the first wife. You will have all due honours. You are not set aside."

"Go," says Djalila.

I hesitate. I have never known Djalila to dismiss me in all these years, since the very first day I came to her. Usually she asks where I am going when I leave her rooms, as though to keep me with her always. She does not even like it when I am gone too long in the souks.

"Go," says Djalila, her voice sunken to a whisper.

I go. I do not know what to do with myself. I make my way to the kitchen where the servants all stop speaking as soon as they see me. I inform Hayfa, while the others pretend to get on with chores, that her master will be taking a new wife. That she is to be shown all due courtesy but that Djalila is still his first wife and that she must be treated with honour. I designate rooms that are to be set aside for Imen and order them cleaned and prepared for her arrival. I tell Hayfa that Ibrahim will send new hangings and carpets for her but that any other comforts are in Hayfa's hands and that she has Ibrahim's permission to purchase whatever is necessary to ensure a warm welcome for Imen when she joins us. I warn Zaynab's nursemaid, Myriam, of the impending changes but I cannot bring myself to tell the child myself. She will find out soon enough and I can only hope that it is a welcome surprise for her once she meets Imen. Meanwhile Djalila keeps away from me, she dismisses me from her presence without reason, she asks for other members of the household to serve her and I wander the rooms like a lost child, searching for peace and finding none.

The engagement rituals must be enacted. The house lies in readiness, the whole family has fine new robes. From today Imen will be promised to Ibrahim and her arrival here will be measured in days.

"I will serve her myself," I tell the slave girl whom Djalila has asked for, a mute who only nods and shrinks away from me.

I make my way into the room and stop in horror. Djalila stands naked, her back to me. In her hands she holds a thin strip of leather, which she brings down suddenly across her thighs, the whip-crack making me startle. At my gasp she turns to face me. Red weals are spread across her arms and legs, her belly. There is even one on her neck.

"What are you doing?" I ask, my voice strangled.

"It takes away the pain," she says.

"What pain?"

"*What* pain?" she says, half-laughing in a way I find more frightening than the red marks across her body. "The pain of this day. Of being set aside for a younger, more beautiful woman. Of being a failed wife."

I step closer, hold out my hand for the leather strip, which she clutches to her. "You cannot do this," I tell her. "You must attend the engagement and you cannot be seen with these marks." I begin to dress her as though everything is normal, although my hands are shaking. I lift up the elaborately decorated robes I have chosen, the heavy jewellery, there to give her confidence but which now must also hide the marks on her body. Slowly I pull the leather from her hands and let it fall to the floor.

"I cannot bear it," she says and tears flow down her cheeks. "Make it stop, Hela. Make it stop."

"It is too late for that now," I say. "If he has another wife you will not need to have him in your bed. You will always be the first wife, you can continue as mistress of the house. Imen will provide sons for Ibrahim…" I have to stop for a moment, for my own voice is trembling too much to speak clearly, "…and all will be well."

"You are shaking," she tells me.

I hear bleating from the courtyard and know that the servants are standing ready with the traditional engagement gifts, which Ibrahim must take to Imen's family. A live sheep and a large jewellery box. Dried fruits and the engagement cake.

"We have to go," I tell Djalila. I pull up the robe on her shoulder so that the red mark there cannot be seen.

"Why are you shaking?" she asks.

"They will be waiting. We need to go." I tell her.

I try not to look at Ibrahim. He is so handsome, dressed in his finest robes. I clench my hands into fists and call too loudly for Myriam to hurry up, where is Zaynab?

Myriam is flustered, she leads down Zaynab, dressed in new robes. Zaynab looks fearful and confused. I want to embrace her, to promise that all will be well but how can I know that, much less promise it to a child?

"We are come to ask if you will give your daughter to be married to Ibrahim an-Nafzawi!"

The crowd cheers and I feel Djalila's grip tighten on mine. Somewhere behind us, Zaynab is being buffeted by the crowd, too small to see what is going on. I want to pick her up and leave this place but instead I stay by Djalila as the ceremony goes ahead and blessings are read over the bowed heads of Imen and Ibrahim. It is too late now, too late.

Standing at Ibrahim's side, Imen is tiny. I am not sure she is much taller than ten-year-old Zaynab and her feet and hands are smaller. She has a little waist but plump cheeks and a rounded behind which speak, one day, of a woman who will grow pleasantly fat on good food. She reminds me of Ibrahim's sisters, their good-natured greed for sweets and gossip, their generous embraces and dimples. Djalila's face is a mask-smile set in stone and yet Imen smiles, smiles at everyone and everything until even Ibrahim's lips have to curve to meet her happiness.

I cannot keep away, do not keep away. I let myself into Ibrahim's bedroom and hear him take her, hear her little cries and his deep groans as he thrusts within her, watch his hands grip her soft flesh and his lips close around her dark nipples. I see her eyes close and her mouth open to receive him, see her own hands grasp him and pull him more tightly to her, as though she cannot get enough of him. I hear their loving whispers one to another and I want to block up my ears so that I may not hear what hurts me.

In the mornings he orders warm breads and sweet honey and feeds her from his own fingers until her kisses drive him to desire. They are insatiable the two of them: she, shown what it is to desire for the first time in her life, he, finding for the first time a woman who openly desires him, who begs for more, who gasps and cries out at his touch, who does not hold back from his need for her, who loves him even as he loves her. Their nights torment me, their days apart when he must work torment the two of them. Imen spends her days in a sun-shined daze of exhausted, contented lust while Djalila retreats ever more from what she does not understand, from what she is only able to resent.

Imen is kind to Zaynab and in return Zaynab, who has never known true kindness, emerges like a flower from a bud. She stops running wild with the street children of Kairouan and instead spends time at home. Her face shines when she is with Imen, she draws closer and closer to her until she will lay her head in Imen's lap as the lazy afternoons drag on and kiss her cheek each morning. She chatters to Imen as though she were her friend, asks her endless questions and listens to the answers as though Imen were the fount of all wisdom. I hear her sing sometimes, her usually quiet voice set free by love.

Even the servants change. They cannot wait to please their new mistress. They do not wait to be commanded, instead they hurry to serve her, to receive her gentle smiles and soft words of thanks. The house seems to become merry. New planters of flowers are brought into the courtyard, a larger fountain is built. The table is laid with new dishes, made to please Imen's appetite. I see changes in the bedrooms, where decorative flourishes are ordered by Ibrahim: more beautiful rugs from his workshops, finer blankets with brighter colours, new carvings and paintings commissioned for the doors and ceilings.

Only Djalila stays locked in her cold world, her fearful place. I think perhaps she could be made to love Imen but she is afraid. She fears Imen's openness as others would fear the sun shining in their eyes – a dazzling light too far away from her own capabilities. She cannot see a way to bridge so great a distance and so she hides away. And perhaps somewhere inside she loved Ibrahim and something in her warmed to his gaze, his touch, but she had locked herself away so tightly she did not know how to open up to him and now she sees she has missed her chance.

It does not take long before Imen finds out something of my past.

"The servants say you are a great healer," she says.

I almost drop the cup of water I am holding. "Who told you that?"

"All of them," smiles Imen.

I shake my head. "I do not practice now," I tell her. "That was a long time ago."

She looks surprised. "You are not that old," she giggles. "Why do you no longer use your skills?"

"I found a new way to serve," I say to her.

"I thought you might give me something," she says, confidingly. "Something to bring me a child."

"A child?"

She laughs. "Why so surprised? Of course, a child. For Ibrahim, he would be so happy."

"You are young," I stumble over my words. "You – you will not need anyone's help to conceive a child."

"A little help never hurt," she smiles at me.

I offer her the red cup at arm's length. I try not to think, nor feel, while I mix what will bring a child. Let her own desire work on it, not my own.

I see her with Zaynab, giggling over the antics of a cat, peering over the rooftops while they munch on sweet pastries and drink fresh juices. I see Zaynab's little heart open up to this, the first person to show her real love and kindness, day after day. It makes my heart sting. I love you too, I want to say to her, I love you, but I am afraid to let it show, I am afraid of what I do to those around me. I swallow and look away when I see them happy together. I wish I could join them, hold Zaynab's warm little body and hug her to me, laugh with Imen over nonsense, relish the warm sun on my skin in the company of people who have some faith in life. Instead I lower my eyes and return to the silence of Djalila's rooms where I continue to shield her from a world that means her no harm but which she has designated her enemy.

It is dark when I hear her retch. I listen again but I do not need to hear that sound a second time. I turn my face to the wall, pull the blanket over my face and weep.

Imen's belly swells in the sun, a ripening that foretells happiness for her, for Ibrahim, even for Zaynab who is enchanted with the idea of a sibling. I see the growing curve beneath her robes and look away, conscious only of a gathering storm. There is a darkness growing even as the light comes, its equal and opposite shadow. I know that Djalila is unhappy, the red weals on her skin emerge with ever greater regularity and not all my pleading will turn her from what gives her relief. Meanwhile Imen drinks daily from the red cup and beams at me, certain that it is I who have helped her fall with child.

It is night when I hear a scraping sound from Djalila's rooms. I make my way to her in the shadows, my feet stepping according to memory rather than sight. I reach out one hand and push at the door, remain in the doorway while I watch her.

She kneels in the pool of light cast by a lantern. Her arms are red with weals from wrist to armpit. One hand works frantically, grinding a substance, the other holds the red cup still.

"The cup is mine," I tell her.

"I have need of it," she says.

"For yourself?"

She keeps grinding.

"You do not know what it does," I tell her. "You cannot use it."

"You put a child in her belly," she tells me, her words emerging in little pants.

"Ibrahim put a child in her belly, whether you wish to hear it or not," I say.

She shakes her head but does not stop grinding. A drop of sweat trickles down her face but she does not wipe it away.

For the second time in my life I throw the cup. Even while it is in the air I pray for it to break, but it does not. Its dark wood is too sturdy, the hard sound it makes as it hits the tiled floor echoes around us and I leave the room so that I do not have to hear Djalila's sobs, nor stifle my own.

But I should have taken the cup and cast it in the sea, thrown it into the desert's sands, buried it in some dark place.

I waken to Hayfa's rough grasp on my shoulder, my whole body shaking under her desperation.

"What," I begin but she has half-pulled me to my feet before I am ready to stand. I stagger.

"The master calls for you," she says.

"It is still dark," I protest.

"The young mistress is bleeding," pants Hayfa.

I run.

I try. I try the cup, but my fear is so great when I set it to Imen's lips that I think all she receives from me is more fear to add to her own. I try to change her position while all around me the whole household kneels in silent prayer. In the silence I watch her life leave and know that Ibrahim's son goes with her.

Darkness falls over our house. Ibrahim's arms are empty. Djalila's heart has been shown to be broken past repair. I dare not love. And Zaynab is growing, growing ever more like her mother in beauty, but without a mother's love.

And five long years pass.

Yusuf

*I*F DJALILA ATTENDED MORE TO what goes on in her own household she would have seen her fifteen-year-old daughter fall in love. No-one with eyes could miss it once it happened, though none of us saw what sparked it. Something happened between them, something none of us saw.

The household is accustomed to receiving guests. A merchant of fine carpets must welcome many men to his home, offer them good food and drink, speak with them on various matters. They must feel cared for in luxurious surroundings and then they will associate that care with the wares they are shown. They will see the beautiful carpets and believe that if they were laid in their own homes they would receive such care, enjoy such luxury always. Djalila's presence only enhances such thoughts. Perhaps, think the men, if their own home were filled with such carpets their own wives would be as beautiful. They are fools to be swayed by so little but traders have always had their ways of making fools of men.

Yusuf is good looking, with black curls and dark eyes, his arms wiry with strength. I hear more than one slave girl sigh at the sight of him on that first night, but Zaynab does not join us for dinner and so when she descends the next morning, her skin rose-blushed and dressed in finery more suited to a celebration than the family table her father looks bemused. I watch her face. She does not look at Yusuf but every part of her being is focused on him, she looks away so hard she might as well raise her eyes and gaze on him without shame. She must have glimpsed him last night but I cannot think when.

His name is Yusuf bin Ali, the chief of the Wurika and Aylana tribes, whose boundaries come close to the great city of Aghmat, far to the west from here. His home is a *ksar*, a fortified city built by desert-dwellers. It is for himself that he comes to buy carpets, but he is a loyal and trusted vassal of King Luqut, the amir of Aghmat and so if he should like Ibrahim's carpets it may well be that we can expect patronage from the amir also.

There are gatherings, some for business, others for pleasure, and Yusuf is our guest at all of them. Some of the evenings are of interest, at others I have to listen to interminable debates about whether or not our rulers are likely to switch their allegiance to Baghdad and what the consequences of that might be. I watch Djalila's face but she is too experienced at these events by now, she keeps her face calm and pleasant, smiles when anyone addresses her and otherwise is silent. I try to stifle my yawns when they speak of politics and hope that one of the scholars will speak of something more interesting.

At first I think it is only Zaynab who feels anything for

him, a young girl a little too admiring of a handsome older man. But Yusuf stays more nights than he had originally planned and I see that he does not turn his head when she enters a room, he seems otherwise engaged. I see his nostrils flare when she walks past him and although he does not watch her go he breathes in her scent as she passes and his eyes close for a brief second. He lusts for her, he cannot help himself. He is too conscious of the curve of her body, the sway of her walk. At one gathering I find myself standing briefly between them. I feel the heat rising between their bodies and words as yet unspoken forming in their mouths, waiting to be heard. But there is something else there too, a kind of helpless tenderness from him for a girl caught in her first love. Somehow they have spoken, he has found out what she feels for him. It does not take long before Yusuf asks a question, a feeling-out of whether Zaynab's hand might be granted.

Ibrahim dismisses the idea. "He has a wife already," he says.

"Zaynab is in love with him," I say.

Ibrahim turns his face away. "We do not always get what we want," he says and my heart sinks at the bitterness in his voice, a bitterness he never had before and for which I hold myself responsible.

"Zaynab could love and be loved," I say. "At least one of us could."

He meets my gaze then and I see that his eyes shine with unshed tears. "So be it," he says. "At least one of us should know what that feels like."

I wait until Yusuf leaves the dining room and heads to bed and I intercept him on the stairs.

"I would speak with you of Zaynab," I say and I watch his face, see his colour change a little, his eyes narrow on my face.

"You are her mother's handmaiden," he says. He does not say *what right have you to speak of Zaynab's marriage*, but I see it in his eyes.

"I am her mother's voice," I say.

He looks me over and does not reply, but he waits to hear what I have to say.

"Did you speak with Zaynab before you spoke with her father?" I ask and I am close enough that I feel the rush of tenderness when he thinks of speaking with her. It is not quite love, no. It is something more than simple lust, though. There is a tightness in him when he thinks of her. I almost want to reach out and touch him, to feel what he feels better, to bring it into focus so that I can name it.

"I have spoken with her," he admits.

"She wants to marry you?"

He only nods. Again the rush, the emotion when he thinks of whatever she said. She has made her feelings for him known, that much I can be sure of. Perhaps he found her charming and no more and then she said something. Few men could feel nothing at all if a beautiful young girl confessed her love for them. And Zaynab is burning up for him, she would have confessed it passionately, unable to hold herself back and in so doing she has secured this feeling for herself, not quite love but close enough that he considers marriage to her.

"You already have a wife though," I say and suddenly

his feelings change to something so dark that I step back. "You have a wife?" I repeat but this time I am questioning him. From the darkness I have just felt I would not be surprised if he had murdered her.

"She is not a well woman," he says and his voice is heavy, his shoulders drop. "She became unwell after the birth of our son. She was sunk in sadness, nothing we could do would pull her back."

I nod. I have seen such women. "She did not recover?" I ask. Usually they do, although with some it may take a long time.

He shakes his head. "We have five sons," he says. "And none has brought her joy."

"She should not birth more children," I say.

"I know," he says. "I no longer lie with her."

I nod. It is becoming clearer to me. He has a wife in name only. A wife sunken in sadness, a wife he may not lie with. He is alone. And here is Zaynab, beautiful as her mother, full of passion and desire, who offers up her love for him like a rare and precious fruit to be plucked at will. What man could resist? For a moment I think of lovely Imen, so trusting in love and then I put the thought away.

"You will be good to her," I say. It is not a question.

"I would protect her with my life," he says and I nod and walk away.

"She should be told," says Djalila stubbornly.

"Let her find out," I tell her. "What use to burden her with such knowledge?"

"And when she sees the other wife? Then what?"

I shake my head. "There is something wrong with the other wife. She barely stirs from her room. Zaynab will have Yusuf to herself."

"It is not nothing to live with another wife," says Djalila. "What would you know of it? It eats away at your soul."

"Plenty of women manage it," I tell her sharply. "It is time you grew up, Djalila. How much pain do you intend to bring to Ibrahim's life?"

Her face goes pale. I curse myself for my lack of control. She will whip herself again and it will be me who has to tend the weals, coax her back to something approaching normality. I follow her, snapping at servants along the way who have done nothing to deserve my anger. In my prayers I think of Zaynab and I feel some relief. Yes, there is another wife but she is ailing in some way. Zaynab loves Yusuf so greatly that her love will draw him towards her, as it has already done. What man can resist such devotion, such passion? He is already filled with tenderness for her and she is too beautiful not to be desired. It is a short step from tenderness and desire to love, she will make him her own eventually. At least I have made one person in this family happy and I feel a little of my burden lift.

The wedding is rushed. Yusuf needs to return to his people. Djalila shuts herself up in her rooms and appears only when necessary. Ibrahim leaves everything to me. And so my memory of those days is of a whirlwind of rituals and robes, of the golden headdress atop Zaynab's flowing hair, of an endless train of camels ready to leave this place. Above all of Zaynab's ecstasy, her happiness so great that the whole house feels it, reels back from its shining force.

In the end it is only Ibrahim who is brave enough to tell the truth, when there is no longer a choice to be made. I see him speak to Zaynab as he bids her farewell and watch her face grow pale. It is too late, she is lifted into the saddle of her camel and when she turn to look back at us, her still-childish face asking an unspoken question, each of us looks away until she is lost to our sight.

In the darkness of the house that night I kneel and beg Allah to care for Zaynab. I have nothing to offer in return, only the misery of this household in return for her happiness.

Kairouan

PERHAPS WE GROW USED TO darkness, to loss. Ibrahim takes his pleasures elsewhere, I do not enquire where and he does not tell me. Djalila I manage as best I can and sometimes her best is good enough for something close to happiness to be felt in the household. The servants know themselves to be lucky, for they are underused, and so they care for the three of us well and manage their own affairs behind closed doors. No doubt they are growing lazy, but I do not care.

Often I walk in the souks, sometimes to seek out traders of medicinal herbs and speak with them. I do not often buy their goods, for I use only a few, but they still respect me and ask for my advice on quality and freshness, on the best uses and care in preserving their goods and it soothes me to speak of healing.

Sometimes I pass by the house that used to be my childhood home. My parents have both gone now, my father died suddenly with a pain in his heart and my grieving mother followed not long after. I had seen little of them, over the years. They never failed to ask me when I would return home and I always replied that my vow was not yet complete. I saw their sad confusion at the turn my life had taken but could not think how to explain what had happened, it seemed too long ago now.

More often I only wander the streets, watch children at play and women gossiping, men bartering. I inhale their lives as others might inhale a perfume, relishing their light-heartedness, their small concerns and greater joys. I am thirty-five, unmarried, still promised to a vow I made when I was only eighteen. I do not seek to escape that vow but I sometimes wonder what my life would have been without it. But I put it away from me, for what other options do I have now? Instead I try to find peace in the life of Kairouan, in its daily rhythms and the changing seasons: sunlight, a cool breeze, the welcome rain after the hot months. I listen to the conversations around me, allowing them to flow over me without attending greatly to what they say. As predicted, our Amir, Al-Muizz, has shifted allegiance from the Fatimids, in part perhaps because of their excessive tributary demands of one million gold dinars a year. Now he has sworn a new allegiance to the Abbasids of Baghdad.

"The Caliph is enraged," says one man.

"What can he do?" asks another.

"Don't speak too lightly," warns the first. "If he were to send the Bedouin tribes here in revenge?"

I wander on. Kairouan is a rich and powerful city, it can withstand almost anything. I do not want to hear of the squabbles of one king and another, I walk here to listen to happier topics. I make my way towards the central square, where a storyteller is surrounded by an eager crowd of men and boys. Women rarely stop to listen but I like his stories of old myths and legends, stories of princesses and djinns. I move closer.

"Then the lady Zaynab's vision came true and her husband Yusuf gave her up!"

There are many Yusufs. There are many Zaynabs. But my breath comes a little faster.

"The King of Aghmat heard of Zaynab's vision and he commanded his vassal Yusuf to give up his bride, that he might be the most powerful man in all of the Maghreb."

My hands are clenched. Aghmat is close to Yusuf's territory. Yusuf is the King of Aghmat's vassal. What is this I am hearing?

I walk into the circle and the storyteller stops, confounded. "I am telling a tale, woman," he berates me. "Be off with you."

I face him, paying no attention to the grumblings around me. "These are yours," I tell him, slipping silver coins into his hand. "Follow me to somewhere quiet and repeat the story you were just telling."

Afterwards I sit, my head aching. How is this possible? He told me that Zaynab had some kind of vision. She claimed that she would be the wife of the most powerful man in the Mahgreb. This in itself is strange enough. Zaynab does not have such powers, I would have felt them in her. What, then, has really occurred? I do not know and there is no way to find out. What happened next then, is that King Luqut of Aghmat decided that her vision was interesting enough that he wanted her for his own bride. He commanded Yusuf to give her up and Yusuf – I curse him in my mind for this – gave her up as ordered. What did he think he was doing? What of his vows to protect her with his life? Zaynab, barely sixteen, married for only one year to Yusuf, is now the queen of Aghmat, torn away from a man whom she loved with a passion so hot it burned me to feel it. The storyteller tells me she screamed when Yusuf told her what was to happen. I wish this was only his embellishment but I fear it is true.

I walk the streets again but now my mind is swirling. I do not see what is around me but my feet know me better than I know myself.

"Hela."

"Moez."

I stand still, in front of him. I do not look at the contents of his stall, do not speak of this and that, do not smile. Perhaps this strangeness in me gives him courage to say what he has waited all this time to say.

"I do not have hundreds of camels," he says. "I have only five, for you know that what I carry is light and small. I am not a rich man, for I serve only certain customers, those whose skills are such that they know what to ask me for."

I say nothing. A brown camel, tethered close by, whooshes in my ear and I stroke its velvet nose without looking at it, my thoughts elsewhere.

"But I am not a poor man," says Moez. "I can offer you a comfortable home, a chance to practice your healing skills."

He waits for me to answer but I stay silent, gazing at him as though I cannot hear what he is saying.

He looks down and I see some colour in his cheeks before he raises his gaze to mine again. "And – and a man who cares for you," he says. "I think of you often, Hela, with tenderness." He swallows a little. "With love," he adds, his voice grown thick.

He did not need to say this. I have felt it for a long time, perhaps for years, unfurling in him slowly, a kindliness, a friendship, then something more, a waiting for me, a nervous excitement when he sees me approaching. He has been slow to recognise his own emotions, slow to name them for what they are. And I think, perhaps I could love this man, perhaps his slowness would slow my own passions, would lead me to a gentler love that I need not fear the consequences of, that I could relax into, knowing comfort rather than anxiety. Perhaps my vow to Allah was nonsense after all, the frightened prayer of a young girl too foolish to accept Faheem's death as His will, proud enough to claim it as her own doing. And the slave boy – it was an accident, nothing more. Why have I bound myself to misery when I could find happiness? Zaynab's story is her own to fashion, Ibrahim and Djalila's stories are also their own. Perhaps all is only the will of Allah and I have no great powers to be fearful of.

I stand silent before Moez and then I hold out my hand to him and he takes it in his own. We stand for a moment.

"Will you come with me on my next journey?" he asks. "It is a trading journey, away from Kairouan, but my mother lives in the countryside now and I would ask for her blessing before we marry."

"Yes," I say.

"We will be away for a month," he says.

"Yes," I say.

"We must leave at dawn tomorrow," he says and I only

nod before I walk away, my heart thumping even though I try to quiet it.

"Away where?" asks Ibrahim.

"With a trader, to look at new healing herbs," I say. I am not ready to tell Ibrahim, I do not have the words.

"A month?" says Djalila and I see her hands begin to clench and unclench. I know that the leather strip is not far from her mind, even though it has been a long time since she has used it.

"I will return," I say, but I do not tell her that I intend to marry Moez, that this journey is in part to receive his mother's blessing for our union.

Hayfa nods, uncertain. "Who is to give orders?" she asks.

"Djalila," I say. In my new hope for the future I think that perhaps I have cocooned Djalila too much. Perhaps if I had not been here all these years she would have had to build her own relationship with Ibrahim rather than through me. Perhaps she would have had to give orders to Hayfa, like every wealthy woman who runs a large household. Perhaps in my absence she will find her voice to order what she wants and maybe she will grow up at last. I have kept her a child and she is no child, she is the same age as I am. Maybe this journey will be a new beginning for us all. There is no reason why she and Ibrahim cannot find some small kind of happiness together that goes beyond the careful courtesy they each employ with one another.

I leave at dawn, taking little with me. A few silver coins, a couple of changes of clothes. Moez has promised me a camel to ride on. Djalila weeps in her room but I bid her a brisk farewell as though she were smiling and I nod to Hayfa, who stands silent in the doorway of her kitchen to watch me go. Ibrahim has already left a little while before me and I am glad of it, there is no need for elaborate farewells when I will return soon enough. There will be enough of all that when I leave this house for good.

I have never been free. I was a child when I left my parents' house. Since then I have been bound by an oath that has made me progressively more unhappy. Now I sit on the warm back of a good-natured nut-brown camel and feel the breeze and the sun on my face. Ahead, Moez rides his own camel, a strong beast taller than my own, a pale sandy colour. Occasionally he looks back at me and when he does I smile and his face lightens with joy. There is little noise about us, the soft pad-pad of the camels' steps, the rustle of tree leaves and birdsong. Occasionally a farmer in his fields or a fellow merchant heading to Kairouan will call out a greeting.

In the hottest part of the day we rest for a while under an olive tree and Moez offers me meat and bread, dates and almonds, fresh water. I think that in all the years in Ibrahim's house, where food is plentiful and elaborate, I have not eaten as well as this. I chuckle a little at the thought of Hayfa's face were I to tell her such a thing, she would take offence when her cooking is some of the best in

Kairouan, her dainty sweetmeats and well-seasoned dishes of meat being dismissed for such simple fare.

"What makes you laugh?" asks Moez.

"I have been foolish," I tell him. "I have waited too long to live my own life."

He does not laugh. He only nods. "I waited too long to speak with you," he says.

I shake my head. "I would not have heard your words before," I tell him. "You spoke when I could hear you."

We are silent for a while, the cool shade of the tree above us providing respite from the worst heat of the day. After a while Moez lays his head in my lap and I stroke his hair.

We go no further than this. Sometimes it is my head in his lap, sometimes his in mine. We do not kiss, we only enjoy the quietness of our closeness. I have not known this before, this trust and gentleness. When the day comes to meet Moez's mother, I kneel willingly before her to ask for a blessing and my smile is so broad that she laughs at me and tells Moez that he has waited too long to marry such a merry woman.

We stay away longer than the month I promised. I do not want to leave this place, this tiny village, hidden in the fold of a valley, protected by the mountains all around us. Perhaps Kairouan's noise and smell, its boldness and greatness, has lost its magic for me. I picture myself living here instead, a healer using only what herbs come to hand, of service to those who need my help, the red cup left behind in Ibrahim's house, to grow dusty without use.

"We could stay here," I say tentatively to Moez.

"You would not be bored?" he asks.

I shake my head.

He smiles. "I might have to travel away from you, to trade, from time to time," he says.

"You would return to me," I say.

"I would," he says and it is a solemn promise.

We will have to return to Kairouan, of course, to make our farewells, to gather our belongings, to plan a new life together.

"But not yet," I beg and he smiles.

It is a trader who brings the news that Kairouan has been attacked. He escaped the worst of it and fled here, to his family's home village. Half his face is mottled with bruises.

"Attacked?" I ask. "What do you mean, attacked?"

"The Zirids shifted allegiance to Baghdad," he begins.

"That happened months ago," I say.

"The Fatimids' Caliph sent the Bedouin tribes to humble Kairouan."

"Humble it?" I think of the vastness of the city, of its power and wealth and cannot imagine what could humble it.

"They targeted the traders, the souks, the marketplace, for they are what makes Kairouan rich. There were hundreds, perhaps thousands of horsemen, each armed with long lances and sharp daggers. The fine leathers of the tanneries were slashed with knives, the carpets were burnt, the copper pots thrown into the furnaces to lose their beaten shapes and return them to a molten, useless mass."

"Did no-one fight them?" I ask, outraged.

"Those who tried were killed. They were without mercy. Women hid in fear of their honour and their lives, even children were not safe. When night fell the city lay in darkness, all of us cowering in our homes, too afraid to light lanterns in case it drew unwanted attention."

The man takes a shuddering breath and the villagers, gathered around, breath with him.

"And then?" I prompt him.

"We believed the destruction to be complete. They had killed so many, ruined so many livelihoods. Surely it was enough for the Caliph. But in the darkest part of the night certain parts of the city were set alight and many houses burnt to the ground. The smoke choked most of the inhabitants in their sleep."

I feel the fear rising from him even as he speaks, can smell the stink of it even before tears begin to roll down his face. My own fear is so strong I am not even sure the smell of it is not coming from me, from my own body.

"The streets were filled with wailing and screams. Children wandered lost and afraid, animals bleated and brayed. In the shadows men turned on one another and fought, unsure if they were breaking the bones of a stranger or their neighbour, too afraid to pause to find out. By the dawn half the city was on fire and the warriors rode through the streets again, killing anyone they saw. Those who could, escaped the city. Some managed to make their way to a mosque and claim sanctuary, although I do not know if it will be granted once they leave its sacred space."

His family lead the man away to rest, his shoulders heaving.

Moez sits down beside me and puts his arm about my waist. "I cannot believe this has happened," he murmurs. "We will wait before we go there, until it is safe to do so. And we will return here, to live simply, as we planned."

But I am shaking my head. "This is my fault," I say, my face white, my hands cold.

Moez frowns. "What do you mean?"

"I broke my vow," I whisper. "I made a vow to Allah when I was eighteen to atone for a sinful deed and I broke it. I was selfish, thinking only of my own happiness. And He has shown me his displeasure."

Moez turns me to look at him. "Are you mad, Hela?" he asks. "You think breaking a vow you made when you were hardly more than a child has led to the destruction of Kairouan?"

I look into his eyes, his worried gaze. "Yes," I say.

At first he utterly refuses my request to return to Kairouan. "It is not safe, Hela, do you not understand this?" he asks, his usual soft voice rising almost to a shout at my stubborn insistence.

I kneel before his mother. "I ask for your forgiveness," I say. "I am unworthy to be your son's wife. I must go."

"We must not be so proud as to believe that we are the only person of importance to Allah," she says softly. "Hela, I do not know what your vow was, but this destruction – it is our rulers' making, not yours."

I bow my head to her, then rise and leave her home. "I will walk if you will not come with me," I tell Moez.

He does not allow that, of course. We make our way back to Kairouan with only two camels, passing day by day the places where we were once happy. We eat but I do not taste it, we sleep but I toss and turn, then wake when it is still night and beg Moez to continue our journey even in the darkness.

At first we see nothing out of the ordinary, after all we are many days' travel from Kairouan. But when only two days separate us from the city we see the blackened fields where crops and even ancient olive trees have been burnt. We see the city in the distance, smoke plumes still rising from it. We meet more and more people heading away from the city walls, their belongings bundled on carts and camels, mules and donkeys, even on their backs if they have no other means. Their faces are drawn in fear and they do not stop to talk, to tell us more than we already know. We gather only that the warriors of the Banu Hilal and Banu Sulaym tribes still roam the streets, the sharp clatter of their horses' hooves the only bold sound left in a city that cowers and creeps, that huddles in fear.

We leave the camels outside the city walls and make our way in through one of the minor gates. We walk the silent streets, the smell of rotting flesh and smoke thick in our nostrils. I hear Moez retch behind me when we pass a corpse but my eyes are fixed straight ahead. We take care to stick to the side streets and even so we see the invaders pass by a few times, their white robes bright in the sun's glare, their faces fierce. We cower against the walls but they do not care about us, we are too abject to be worthy of their attention now that the city is on its knees before them.

Ibrahim's workshops have been burnt to the ground, the wooden doors gone, with only metal hinges to show where they should hang. I walk through them, my feet sinking in ashes as little scraps of burnt paper patterns and wool float past on the wind.

"Why are we here?" asks Moez.

Because I am afraid to go to the house, I think. *Because people may have escaped from their place of work, but from their own house? Because I am a coward.* I do not speak, only walk away from the workshops and towards home.

The street is silent and the door that leads to Ibrahim's house is gone, fallen into ash.

Moez grips my arm. "Enough," he says. "I ask you not to enter."

I turn to face him and I do not even need to speak.

He steps back from me. "I will be waiting," he says. "Where my shop was, if it is still there – and even if it is not. I will wait for however long it takes."

I do not answer him. I hear his footsteps fade away before I enter the courtyard, where there was once a fountain and a garden.

I do not run or scream. I walk one slow step at a time, as though if I move faster I will not see the full horror of what is before me. I do not scream, I whisper, as though I am afraid of receiving an answer. I breathe in the smell of smoke and I choke out the names of the servants. No-one replies. I stand in silence outside Ibrahim's room and it takes me a long time to raise my hand and push against the charred wood.

I do not enter the room, do not kneel by the side of what I see there, the shape of what used to be a man. I look and then I close my eyes and know that I will never again close my eyes without seeing what I have seen here.

I walk through Djalila's rooms. The metal birdcages sway in the breeze that comes when I open the door and ashes drift in low clouds across the floor with each step that I take. I pause by one cage to touch the black feathers that were once bright yellow and the tiny outstretched wingtip crumbles to nothing. I stand by Djalila's bed and address the wall.

"I failed you."

There is no answer, no sound in this dead house except my own voice.

"I killed your brother because I loved him too much," I tell her, as though she can hear me. "I killed him and then I tried to save you, to atone for what I did to him. I thought if I made you happy again that I would be forgiven. Instead I only made more unhappiness."

The wall is silent but I cannot lower my gaze.

"I made a good man unhappy with my arrogance in thinking I could heal you," I say. "I stole your husband without your knowledge because I desired him and lied to myself about what I was doing." The words come in retches, as though I am vomiting up their poison after all these years of suffering in silence. "I killed a young girl and her unborn child because I could not foresee your bitterness at her innocence. I let your daughter grow up without a mother's touch."

I close my eyes and feel the tears seep out from under my eyelids. "I do not know how to make amends," I say. "I do not know how."

I shelter in the ruins for three days and nights, during which time I do not sleep or eat. I drink a little water, when I remember to, from the last dregs of the courtyard pool, dirty with ashes, which should taste bitter in my mouth but I cannot seem to taste anything. I walk from one room to another, each unrecognisable and then I walk them again and then again, as though I might miraculously find a room that is unharmed. I touch scraps of fabric: blankets, hangings, carpets and each falls to pieces between my fingertips leaving only blackness on my skin. Sometimes I sit and allow the sun to shine on me through the broken window shutters until even its distant heat burns my skin. I try to think but really there is nothing in my mind. I cannot summon up the energy to cry or be angry, not even with myself. Occasionally I close my eyes and something like sleep comes to me although it is not a true sleep but rather a darkness which shows me what I have lost and I quickly re-open my eyes that I may not be tormented.

By the third day something like thoughts return to me. I take things from different parts of the house and collect them in what was once Ibrahim's study. I find coins and some unburnt clothes that only smell of smoke, a water bag.

There is a part of me that thinks: I am free now. Those to whom I owed a debt are all dead and the cup that cursed me is gone, burnt to ashes, all the power it had lost. I am free of its draw, its call on me. I can leave Kairouan and return to the mountains with Moez, live as I dreamt of living. But the ashes on my face when I look in Djalila's mirror tell me otherwise, they show me my only possible future.

Zaynab.

I will serve her if she will let me. I will try to make her happy as atonement for her dead uncle, her dead parents, the love she was never given as a child. I have nothing to offer, but I will serve her as she commands.

I kneel for the dawn prayer and rise, collect up my things and slip out of the garden. I will not go to Moez, for I will only cause him more hurt and he would follow me, would try to help me when I must do this alone.

"Hela! *Hela!*"

I turn and see a boy running towards me, a dirty cloth in one hand. The rising sun behind him makes me squint but as he reaches me I see it is the slave boy I once saved, grown almost to a man. Now he stands before me, panting from his run.

"This is for you," he tells me, holding out the cloth.

I take it and unwrap what lies within its folds. My hands are quicker than my mind, they let the cup fall, as though even my fingers are trying to rid me of it, to let it break into a thousand splinters.

But the boy is too quick for me and he catches the cup even as it falls from my grasp. "I saved it from the fire for you," he tells me solemnly. "So that you can save others as you saved me."

Zaynab

*T*HE JOURNEY WEST AND THEN south to Aghmat is a torture to me. My feet blister from the distances I walk. Few people will give a lift to a woman dressed in rags with a vacant face, who smells of smoke. I frighten them. I have a little money to pay for simple food when I find vendors along the way, but not enough for a place to rest my head when the nights fall, so I sleep in fields or ditches by the side of the road. I see the moon grow fat and thin again and my pace slows, for my feet bleed. I could stop somewhere to let them heal but I am afraid that my money will run out. I stick to the main roads, where caravans of traders pass me by with indifference, but their very presence keeps me safe from bandits and allows me to know that I am travelling in the right direction. A few times a trader allows me to sit on one of their carts or on an under-loaded camel and I bless them in a voice that comes out as a croak, I speak so little. They nod warily at the blessing but I can see that my presence makes them uncomfortable and they are glad when they can leave me behind again. When they ask where I am headed I tell them that I am going to Aghmat, to serve the queen there and they raise their eyebrows at the idea of a crone like myself serving Queen Zaynab, famed for her beauty and for the prophecy that her husband will one day command all of the Maghreb.

Aghmat is a famous city, one that grows with every year that passes. It is a stronghold, a shining jewel along the trade routes. It is one of the first stops when traders return over the treacherous mountains from the desert tribes or the Dark Kingdom in the south. It is their last stop to take on water and food before attempting the desert when they bring goods from the far-off lands in the north, across the sea. Caravans of more than a hundred camels are a matter of course here, carrying salt, gold, silver, the finest cloth – not only wool and linen but silks and those which have been embroidered or woven with golden threads. Delicate glass, sturdy metal, carved wood. As I draw closer I am joined by local farmers and traders on the path to the city walls, bearing oranges, sugar cane, little cakes and pastries, live animals for slaughter. Their baskets and carts make me feel faint with hunger. What food I have eaten along the journey has been the cheapest I could buy: stale bread, scraps of vegetables, worm-eaten fruits. No meat, no sweets. My belly has not been full for a long time. As I enter the city I pass many food stalls but I have no money. I must find Zaynab.

At last the gates of the palace rise up above me. I rest for a moment, tears of relief rising up in me.

The guards are unimpressed when I ask for entry.

"You most certainly cannot see the queen," says one, "Be off with you."

"She knows my name," I tell him. "She will reward you for allowing me into her presence."

"I doubt it," says the other one.

I scrabble through my dirty bag and hold out the cup. "Give this to Zaynab and tell her that Hela is here to serve her," I tell the first guard.

"Fuck off," says the guard and he shoves my shoulder so hard that I fall to the ground.

I look up at him and begin to mumble something. It is only the names of plants, of medicines from far away, but he goes pale, for he thinks I am cursing him.

"All right, all right, crone," he says, blustering but afraid. "Give it here."

I have to shuffle into the throne room, for my feet hurt so badly I cannot bear to lift them up and set them down.

She is here. Beautiful beyond words, lovelier than Djalila but somehow just as sad. She looks at me in fear, perhaps because of the news I bring, perhaps because of my appearance. And she feared me anyway, as a child, she could not see that those about her were scarred from love, she only saw that there was no love given to her and so she sought it elsewhere. And her attempt failed somehow, Yusuf has given her to his king, a man broad in the chest and dressed with magnificence but with something about him that I do not like the feel of.

"You will live here, in the palace," decrees Luqut, once I have told him all I know of Zaynab's loss.

"I beg to live quietly in the city," I ask. "But I will willingly serve the Queen." I do not want to be too close to this man, to the darkness that hangs over Zaynab, whatever it is.

Luqut shrugs. "As you wish," he says. "A place will be found for you." He calls over an official, speaks briefly with him, nods.

I wait for Zaynab to speak but she says nothing, she only looks at me with her black eyes.

"You will attend Zaynab this evening," decrees Luqut. He indicates a senior-looking official. "Meanwhile you will follow him to your new home."

I shuffle after him. He walks too fast for my blistered feet but we do not go far from the palace. Just outside its walls is a tiny street, almost hidden.

The official stops outside a blue-painted door. He does not bother to show me in, only indicates it with his chin. "Belongs to the king, he says you are to have it now." He hands me a small pouch, which chinks.

I wait for him to enter the house before me but he is already striding away.

The door is small, old, the blue paint thick in its cracks and crevices, as though it has been painted many times. I push against it and it opens with a shudder.

It is a strange little house. There is dust everywhere and no sign of furniture, as though it has been stripped bare at some point in the past. There are only two rooms, each one a little crooked, the walls not smooth. But it has beautiful tiles on the floor and someone has added carved plasterwork to the uneven ceiling, as though the person who lived here before me was both poor and esteemed. There is a tight staircase, which I follow, its walls rough clay, not even painted, but when I reach the top I find myself standing on a small rooftop terrace. It is empty save for a tattered cloth still clinging to two lopsided wooden poles, the remnants of an awning. I could walk the length and breadth of the space in only five steps either way. I stand for a few moments, looking about me at the rooftops around me. Many are taller than mine of course, I cannot see very far across the city. I retrace my steps back to the dark rooms below and place my small bundle on the floor. I look in the small pouch. The money Luqut has given me is generous. I shuffle my way into the bright light of the afternoon to seek out what items I will have need of here. I find a street boy who I pay well to be my guide in this new place and to carry my purchases: a full water jug, cooking utensils and a small brush for sweeping away the dust, blankets, a fresh robe, a bag in which I can carry my belongings, sandals, a cloth to wrap up my hair. I make arrangements with local tradesmen to make me a simple bed, to deliver a large storage jar for water, firewood, to come and make a new awning on my tiny rooftop. I buy food from the street vendors near the blue house and sit on the doorstep to eat, the boy wolfing his portion down in moments.

"Here," I tell him, passing him another coin. "Buy sweet pastries."

He is gone and back in moments and we eat our fill, honey dripping onto our chins, our fingers sticky. My belly aches with fullness, a pain I am grateful for. I pour a little water on both our hands and we drink it, cold and refreshing. The boy's last task is to take me to the hammam, where I bid him farewell, though I am sure he will loiter about my new home on a regular basis now that he knows me as a potential source of both food and coin.

I stand in the blue doorway. My body is cleaner than it has been for a very long time. My hair is wrapped in a cloth, my robe and shoes are stiff with newness. My feet still hurt but I put a healing balm on them and wrapped them in clean cloths, they will mend. The bag I carry contains a few ingredients I chose from the market and the cup. I did not hesitate to take it with me. It was returned to me at the moment when I accepted my fate, it is a sign. I begin my walk to the palace, for darkness is beginning to fall.

When I arrive Zaynab is surrounded by other servants.

"You may all go," I say.

They look to her for confirmation and she hesitates before nodding. They leave the room looking back over their shoulders. Who am I, to arrive in the morning and become their queen's chosen handmaiden by the evening? I do not pay attention to them. I am used to being regarded with suspicion. Instead I look at Zaynab.

"Why did you come here?" she asks. It is the first time I have heard her voice since she left her parents' home.

"Kairouan burnt to the ground," I say.

"You could have gone anywhere," she says.

"I owe your family a debt," I say.

"What debt?" she asks.

I shake my head. "Should I prepare you for the King?" I ask.

I feel the darkness well up in her. "He will prepare me

himself," she says and walks away, into another room. I follow her.

The edges of this room are dark. Only the centre gleams in the light of lanterns, their red-gold light shining on polished metal, on the surface of well-worn leather, on the silken ripples of Zaynab's long hair. I look at what is laid out here and when Zaynab turns I meet her gaze in silence. Then I hear footsteps and move behind a wall hanging. She watches me hide and says nothing, only turns to face Luqut as he enters the room.

He orders her to undress and she does so, her robes slipping to the ground. He touches her where he has touched her before, admiring his handiwork, the damage he has done to her skin, rubbing a thumb over each bruise and scar as though it brings him pleasure even now. His large hand grips her throat and forces her chin upwards while his other hand bears down on her shoulder. She sinks to her knees before him.

She does not speak when she is spoken to, she does not beg for mercy when he selects his tools. She is strong, she bears what he does to her longer than I would have thought possible before she cries out and when she does I think, *you will die for this, Luqut.*

He leaves her on the floor afterwards, her body crumpled as though she had fallen from some great height. I wait until his footsteps are far away and then I blow out all the lanterns except one and I tend to her in its dimness. She does not weep, she does not speak, only looks at me when I help her to stand.

"I am here now," I say.

I can see that it is not enough, that she does not trust

me, does not believe that my being here can bring about any change in her circumstances. I do not try to convince her. I go over his work with my own, covering each bruise with simple unguents. Now that I am here I will need to make my own, they will be better than the ones I bought in the market. When I am done, I lead her to bed and cover her body with blankets. I ask her a few questions although I am fairly sure of the answers already. I see her eyes well up and think, she is still a child. Married twice, a queen and still a child. I wait for a moment.

"I heard about your vision. Every ambitious man in the Maghreb wanted you for a wife when they heard about it."

I see tears trickling but she does not answer.

"Do you often have visions?"

She does not answer. I already knew it was a lie. I wait in silence for a moment and then I leave her. I pass the servants, the guards. Evidently my name is already known, for no-one bars my way nor questions who I am.

Darkness

I make my way up the rough stairs and reach the roof terrace. I lean my hands on the wall and look out into the darkness, lit here and there with lanterns, before I sit on the bare floor. I take out the cup from my bag and set it before me. And I make a new vow. I may have failed before in what I tried to do but I did not know what I was capable of, I shied away in fear from what was possible. Now I will not hold back from the cup's power. Zaynab's so-called vision may have been the foolish prank of a child crying out for love without knowing the power of what she did but I will make it come true. I have lost everything, there is nothing left to lose.

There will be none such as she, no woman of such beauty or power. Men will lust for her, women will fear her and none will dare harm or stand against her, for I will be at her side. I have been timid and fearful of the powers that I can wield but no longer.

No longer.

For readers

Hela and Zaynab are recurring characters in the rest of my Moroccan series, made up of this novella and three full-length novels, both published and forthcoming.

You can find out more about them as well as other historical series I have written, on my website, www.melissaaddey.com.

Historical notes

Although the settings are as accurate as I could make them at a distance of over a thousand years, Hela herself is an entirely fictional character. While writing my Moroccan trilogy I became fascinated by Hela's backstory. She began as an almost-silent yet powerful woman in the shadows of Zaynab's life and so I ended up writing a prequel novella on Hela's early years.

Zaynab is a real historical character, from Kairouan, Tunisia, a city known for its very fine carpets and rose perfume. Her father was named Ibrahim and she married four times in the course of her life (beginning with Yusuf and then Luqut, the King of Aghmat), eventually becoming the wife of the most powerful man in the Maghreb (North Africa), who created the Almoravid empire, stretching across Morocco and Spain. This apparently fulfilled a vision she had. I tell her story in *None Such as She*, a full-length novel. Her two rivals in love feature in *A String of Silver Beads* and *Do Not Awaken Love*.

After having been a very wealthy and powerful city, Kairouan was attacked in 1057 and more or less ruined for political and religious reasons, although the attacks may have taken place over a longer period. It never really recovered its former importance.

Medicine at this time in the West would have been quite basic but the Islamic world had some very advanced medicinal knowledge and books. Paper was in use.

Biography

I mainly write historical fiction, and am currently writing two series set in very different eras: China in the 1700s and Morocco/Spain in the 1000s. My first novel, *The Fragrant Concubine*, was picked for Editor's Choice by the Historical Novel Society and longlisted for the Mslexia Novel Competition.

In 2016 I was made the Leverhulme Trust Writer in Residence at the British Library, which included writing two books, *Merchandise for Authors* and *The Storytelling Entrepreneur*. You can read more about my non-fiction books on my website.

I am currently studying for a PhD in Creative Writing at the University of Surrey.

I love using my writing to interact with people and run regular workshops at the British Library as well as coaching other writers on a one-to-one basis.

I live in London with my husband and two children.

For more information, visit my website
www.melissaaddey.com

Current and forthcoming books include:

Historical Fiction
China
The Consorts
The Fragrant Concubine
The Garden of Perfect Brightness
The Cold Palace

Morocco
The Cup
A String of Silver Beads
None Such as She
Do Not Awaken Love

Picture Books for Children
Kameko and the Monkey-King

Non-Fiction
The Storytelling Entrepreneur
Merchandise for Authors
The Happy Commuter
100 Things to Do while Breastfeeding

Thanks

My thanks go to Professor Harry Norris and Dr Michael Brett of the School of Oriental and African Studies for their wonderful books on Berbers, Tuaregs and this era as well as their helpful information and encouragement. All mistakes are of course mine.

Thank you to my brother Ben, whose different way of sensing illness is both fascinating and strange to me. It gave me the inspiration for some of Hela's skills, although I think he is a great deal wiser.

Huge gratitude to the University of Surrey for giving me funding for my PhD in Creative Writing, allowing me freedom and valuable writing time for multiple projects over three years. And especially to Dr Paul Vlitos, who has already improved my writing craft with his knowledge and encouragement.

To my beta readers for this book: Camilla, Elisa, Etain and Helen, thank you so much for all your insights and questions as well as your demands for the next book! You make each book better.

And always, my thanks to Ryan, who makes all things possible and to Seth and Isabelle for putting up with Mamma having her head in the clouds.

36959788R00072

Printed in Great Britain
by Amazon